BORN TO BE WILD
THE 8TH CONTINENT

MATT LONDON

razOr
bill
An Imprint of Penguin Random House

THE 8TH CONTINENT

BORN TO BE WILD

BUILD IT.

RUN IT.

RULE IT.

MATT LONDON

An Imprint of Penguin Random House
Penguin.com

ISBN: 978-1-59514-756-1

Printed in the United States of America

1 3 5 7 9 10 8 6 4 2

For my family

RICK LANE WATCHED THE SKY. SOMETHING IN HIS QUICK-THINKING, HYPER-DEVELOPED BRAIN knew—today was going to be a big day.

All around him, workers bustled about his family's settlement, carting wheelbarrows full of dirt and rubble. Four-legged robots hauled sheet metal on their backs. When the wind picked up, Rick tasted the slightly salty ocean air that felt so familiar to his new home, the eighth continent.

The boy stood at the end of his block, where there was an empty and expectant circle of dirt. In the middle of the circle was a deep hole, a foundation, but Rick's eyes never left the cerulean expanse above his head. He considered each cloud, waiting for The Big Day to begin.

"Rick!" A warm, familiar voice called out to him. He turned and saw his mother walking toward him. Beside her was the seven-foot-tall crow 2-Tor, Rick's formerly-a-robot friend and protector, who, on a recent adventure, had been transformed into a real-life talking bird. Such had been the power of the Eden Compound, a chemical substance designed by Rick's father that had also turned the Great Pacific Garbage Patch into this very land that Rick now loved.

2-Tor clacked his beak. "I say, Richard, you are looking quite ready to catch the worm this morning."

"I am, 2-Tor. I am!" Rick pumped his fists in the air, doing a victory dance like the fighters in the video game *Crazy Combat* when they defeated opponents. "It's a big day! You know what's happening today, right?"

"Though my memory banks lack the efficiency of their formerly artificial intelligence, I do seem to recall a certain milestone scheduled for today."

"Is it the anniversary of when we cleaned up the stain?" asked Rick's mother. She was almost right. In a few days it would be six months since Rick and his family had used the eighth continent as a giant sponge to soak up an ink stain floating in the ocean. Governments all over the world had sent letters of appreciation and gifts of gratitude to the Lanes. But that wasn't the big news.

"Nope! That's not it!"

"Well, don't make us guess, honey!" His mom smiled affectionately.

Rick cheered, "Today's the day Dad brings the mansion from Geneva!"

Bang! The door to one of the portable metal buildings that lined the block blew open, and a ten-year-old girl appeared in an oversized T-shirt and nylon shorts. Her black hair was a chaotic mane that she tried to wrestle into a ponytail as she ran barefoot down the dirt road past more sleep shelters, still in her pajamas. "Dad's bringing the house today? Awesome! Is he here yet? Can I see it?"

"Evie, go put on some shoes!" Mom's eyes bulged halfway out of her head. "I'm going to need to disinfect your feet with a mop!"

But Rick's sister, Evie, was not about to turn around for a pair of shoes. She got right up in Rick's face. "Well? Where is he? Why didn't you tell me Dad was coming back today?"

Rick sighed, adjusting his glasses. "I *did* tell you, Evie, like five or six times. But you just don't pay attention. You're always off exploring the jungle instead of helping us around the settlement."

"Nuh-uh! I always pay attention!"

2-Tor cleared his throat. "Actually, Evelyn, I seem to recall Rick mentioning your father's itinerary to you on multiple occasions."

Evie turned. "Sorry, 2-Tor, did you say something?"

2-Tor sighed. "No, miss. Pay this bird no mind at all."

Before they could continue the dispute, the high-pitched whine of hover engines filled Rick's ears. High above them, the *Roost* appeared. Rick had missed his hovership, the flying tree that had gotten him and Evie out of so many jams. It was good to see the old girl again.

But today, the *Roost* had brought a friend. Dangling from long tethers attached to the roots of the tree hung their old home, Lane Mansion. It was a tall, silver house shaped like the outstretched wing of a bird. Morning sunlight glimmered off the building's surface.

Rick couldn't wait to get back in his old room and sleep in his own bed. It would be nice to have the whole family together again, instead of living in their own separate sleep shelters.

Waaaark!!! While the *Roost* hovered above them, a cardinal swooped down from one of the branches of the flying tree and landed at Rick's feet. The bird had the handle of a small pail in its beak.

"Oh, hey, Red!" Rick gave the bird a scratch on top of its head and picked up the pail. "What have you got for us?"

Inside the pail was a black boxy device that looked like a video game controller. Rick recognized it as an infrared piloting remote he had always wanted to get his hands on for its power and versatility. Also in the pail was a handwritten note from his father. He started to unroll the paper, but Evie snatched it out of his hands.

While Mom shouted at her and 2-Tor lectured about keeping her hands to herself, Evie read the note aloud: "Dear kids, I'm home! But unfortunately the nav-computer is totally shot. I was trying to cook some marshmallow taquitos in the microwave and blew out most of the *Roost*'s electrical systems. You'll have to guide me in with this. See you soon! Love, Dad. PS—Do either of you like carbon on your taquitos?"

Rick held tightly to the remote in his hands, partly because he wanted to make his dad proud and partly because he assumed Evie was about to try to snatch the remote away.

"Okay, everyone, stand back." Rick switched on the targeting remote and established a connection with the *Roost*. He pushed on one of the joysticks, and the hovership swayed to the side. Perfect. It responded just like the flightsim video game on his pocket tablet.

"Wait, Rick!" Evie whined. "I want to do it. You always get to do all the cool technical stuff."

"Stop it, Evie. I have the controller."

"Pleeeeeeeeeease!"

"No!"

She reached for him, tickling his ribs. As Rick doubled over giggling, Evie snatched away the controller. She pushed down on the joystick. The *Roost* and mansion dropped like a falling icicle.

"Evie! Give it back."

She gave him an accusing look. "What, don't you trust me?"

"Well, yes, but—"

"Good! Whee!" She played with the controls so that the *Roost* did a soaring lap around the settlement, zooming over the quick-assemble shelters and the heads of the workers. They had built a quaint little village in the six months since they had rooted the eighth continent to the ocean floor, but there was still a lot to do. Buildings needed to be built, farms needed to be farmed, and new technologies to rapidly improve the continent had to be researched. Everyone had a job, even Evie, who hosted meetings to make sure all the workers and scientists had their voices heard. Rick had primarily been working with a team of landscapers to cut away the dense jungles that covered much of the southeastern quarter of the continent, where Professor Doran's fast-forming flora had flourished—a necessary sacrifice to ensure that the settlement had room to grow.

Professor Doran was an old friend and teacher of Rick's parents, and he had helped them root the continent six months ago. He had also brought the seeds for millions of plants to cover the vast, blank surface of the continent with different habitats. Rick missed Professor Doran's supersized plants and funny stories about their parents when they were younger. But most of all he missed the professor's young assistant, Sprout Sanchez. Sprout could hog-tie haricot verts faster than anyone Rick had ever met, and he had set world records on multiple Game Zinger games.

The *Roost* zoomed over Rick's head, buzzing the settlement once more. Evie cackled gleefully. Rick let out an irritated growl. If Sprout had been there to see Evie acting this crazy, he would not have been pleased.

Come to think of it, Sprout would probably be hooting and hollering, asking to have a turn dive-bombing the worker robots with the hanging house.

"Okay, Evie," Rick said, finally having had enough. "Quit playing. We have to lower the mansion into the foundation."

"Fine, fine." Evie brought the *Roost* around for a final

loop of the settlement and returned it to hover mode over the dirt pit.

"Now let me have it," Rick insisted, reaching for the controller.

Evie pushed down hard on the joystick. The hovership dropped a hundred feet and then froze in place. The mansion swung wildly from side to side. Evie said, "No! It's my job. Let me help."

"But I know how to do this!" Rick said.

"So do I!"

"Kids!" Mom shouted over the noisy screams of the two children and the hover engines. "Don't fight."

The *Roost* dropped lower as Evie eased the base of the mansion closer to the foundation. It was nearly in place, but Rick could see that her aim was off. She was lowering the mansion too fast, and she wasn't going to fit it into the hole perfectly. Disaster was about to strike.

"Evie, wait! Give it to me. You're going to mess it up!" Rick grabbed for the controller.

"No!" Evie shrieked and yanked the controller away.

Her hand slipped. The mansion thudded against the side of the foundation. The tethers snapped, and the Lane family's beloved house toppled over like a felled tree. It smashed into the ground and crumbled into many pieces. The metal and rubble and all their family treasures spilled across the dirt like a devastated piñata.

"Look what you did!" Rick and Evie screamed at each other.

"Me? It was *your* fault!" they both retorted.

So angry it looked like her joints had locked, Mom stomped over to Rick and his sister, pried the two apart, ripped the controller from Evie's fingers, and guided the *Roost* to a safe landing nearby. Seconds later, Rick's father, the wide-eyed inventor George Lane, stumbled from the hovership. Mom ran to him and gave him a tight hug.

"Wowza!" he said, mopping the sweat from his brow. "That was quite a ride. And my goodness! I didn't know we had planned to dismantle the house. Smart thinking, Evie. We probably should have done that in the first place."

"Smart thinking?!" Rick felt his face turn as red as his hair. "No, Dad, it was stupid thinking! Evie ruined *everything!*"

"If you had just let me do it, everything would be fine!" Evie's eyes were all watery, and her lip quivered when she yelled.

"It would not have been fine." Rick pressed his advantage. "It wasn't coming down straight. I saw it. Dad, how can you not punish her for messing it all up?"

"I . . . well . . ." Dad scratched his head. "This mess does put us in a bit of a pickle."

Evie looked between the members of her family, giving each one in turn a betrayed stare. "I hate this family! All I want to do is help you, and you resent me for it!"

"No one said we resent you." Mom reached out to her daughter, but Evie turned away and began to storm off, away from the wreckage of Lane Mansion, into the dense jungles of the continent.

"I'm out of here," Evie said, still barefoot and in her pajamas. "I'm done with this family. So I'm leaving. And that, Rick?" She gave him the meanest glare of all. "That *is* your fault."

As they watched Evie disappear into the trees, Dad said, "Come on, Rick. Go after her. Say you're sorry."

Rick snorted. There was no way he was about to do that.

Mom let out a worried sigh. "2-Tor, please follow Evie and make sure she's safe."

"Yes, of course, madame." 2-Tor flapped his wings, taking to the air and soaring over to the tree line where Evie had disappeared.

"Come on, son," Dad said, stepping over to the wreckage of the mansion. "Let's see what we can salvage from this mess."

Rick's stomach was all curled up. He felt sick. It was a big day all right, but not the kind he had hoped for. Was this the day Evie left the Lane family for good?

THE JUNGLE WAS THICK WITH TREES. BRANCHES OBSTRUCTED EVERY PATHWAY, LIKE STRONG ARMS

restraining Evie, telling her to stop and go back. Giant leaves slowed her progress. She pushed them aside. The green portals were like doors to another world. And that's exactly where Evie wanted to go.

Evie had argued with her brother and her parents before, but it felt different this time. There was something final about it, a distressing reality she knew she hadn't fully grasped. In the aftermath of the fight, her heart was still pounding—a ferocious, adrenaline-fueled beating in her chest—like she was running down a steep hill and couldn't slow herself down.

I never fit in with them anyway, Evie thought to herself. Her mom was a critical neat freak. Her brother judged everything she did. He was so competitive, and he never said anything nice. All Rick ever did was point out all the things Evie did wrong.

The accident kept playing over in her mind. She grasped

at the memory, trying to find a way to make it so that it wasn't her fault. Rick had grabbed at the controller. She wanted to blame him, but if she had just landed the *Roost* like she was supposed to, everything would have been fine. Instead, all her family's treasures were smashed, lost in the wreckage of her old home.

Truthfully, that was what hurt most of all—Evie wanted to mourn the loss of Lane Mansion as much as the rest of her family did, but somehow she felt like she couldn't.

Pebbles and roots pricked her bare feet with each step. She really should have put on shoes before storming off. But what kind of message would that have sent? "I hate you! I'm out of here! Wait, first let me go find my hiking boots."

She hadn't seen any wildlife in the jungle today, but that didn't surprise her too much. As soon as Professor Doran's plants had taken root on the surface of the continent, a number of conservation agencies had sent endangered species to live in peace on the huge island. Birds nested. All sorts of creatures had new homes safe from pollution and deforestation. Of course, as soon as Rick needed to widen the perimeter of the Lane settlement, he had started chopping down the trees Professor Doran had planted. No wonder animals had fled the area, seeking refuge in the center of the continent.

Rick's actions made Evie feel like a flock of screeching parakeets had nested in her brain. One of the main reasons they created the eighth continent in the first place was so animals could be safe from the "progress" that had devastated their old habitats. Now all Rick cared about was bringing more scientists and high-tech equipment to his utopia. Evie wanted to build an awesome amusement park inside the world's largest petting zoo, where people and animals could hang out and play together. Parkgoers could ride roller coasters with giraffes and sit with hippos on a waterslide. But no one gave a hoot what Evie wanted. She had pleaded with her family to put it to a vote. Surely there were some people in the settlement who would prefer going on epic adventures to conducting boring research. But her family said no, and the science committee—led by Rick and their father, of course—decided Evie's ideas would not be the objectives of the settlement.

Still brooding and out of breath, Evie reached the base of a steep hill. This was an unpleasant development. Climbing barefoot was not going to be fun.

"At least it's warm out," she said with a sigh.

Lightning lanced across the sky. One deafening thunderclap heralded a downpour that drenched Evie in seconds. Her pajamas clung to her uncomfortably as heavy droplets splashed on her head, easily fighting through the tree cover to torment her. The raindrops were hot. The sky must have been boiling. Evie could relate.

"Evelyn! Please, Miss Evelyn!" a gentle voice cried out from behind her. She turned to see 2-Tor making his way through the trees, pushing branches aside with his beak.

His dark feathers, soaked with rainwater, clumped against his body. Droplets beaded down the cracked TV screen in his belly, the last reminder of his former robot self.

"Go away, 2-Tor! I'm not going back there." She grabbed the trunk of a young tree for support and started pulling herself up the hill. Her foot slipped and she fell, smearing her leg with mud. Undeterred, Evie pressed on, fighting her way to the top.

2-Tor shook out his soggy wings. He was too wet to fly, but the bird was persistent. He followed Evie up the hill. "I must say, miss, you certainly do not make things easy for anyone."

"Yeah," Evie grunted as she used a big brown rock as a stepping-stone. "Then they should be glad to be rid of me. Stupid Evie, always messing everything up."

She slipped again, falling headfirst into the mud. It covered her front completely. "Ugh . . . Ugch . . ."

The big crow caught up to her and slipped his wingtips under her arms. He scooped her up and placed her back on the uneven ground. "What I was trying to say, miss, is that you do not make things easy, but you are worth it. The family needs you. Please come home."

"I said no, 2-Tor!" She angrily shoved the bird, and his talons went out from under him. He landed hard in the mud and tumbled a short way down the hill.

"Evelyn! *Waaark!*"

2-Tor looked so miserable and helpless in the mud. She didn't want to see him like that, so she pushed her way up the last hundred feet of hill and reached the top. Trees did not grow up there. Instead there was a grassy field under the tumultuous sky. Even in the mist and the rain, Evie had an impressive view of the eighth continent. She could see the three big mountain peaks at the center of the continent—Imagination, Perspiration, and Luck. Mount Luck was actually quite close. On the far side of the grassy hilltop, a natural stone bridge extended from the end of the field to a cliff near the base of the mountain. "Near the base" was actually several hundred feet up, and the bridge arched over a fairly deep ravine. Evie wondered what kind of trash had formed the bridge like that before the Eden Compound had turned it to stone.

The rain came down harder on the hilltop, where there were no trees to shield Evie. The water washed most of the mud from her arms and legs as she scurried across the hill and began traversing the bridge. The stone was wet and slippery. She tried to stay in the middle of the bridge, crouching down onto her hands and knees whenever she got dizzy.

"Do not cross that bridge, Miss Evelyn!" 2-Tor pleaded from behind her. His feathers were caked with dark brown mud that stuck to his beak. The big bird looked quite miserable but committed to his mission.

"2-Tor, go home! It's not safe for you out here!"

"Nor you, dear girl!" The bird started after her across the bridge.

Evie picked up her pace. She didn't know how else to get

the message into his bird brain. She wasn't going to be part of Rick's scitopia anymore.

When Evie was nearly across, 2-Tor let out a desperate squawk. He had slipped on the wet stone and fallen. The bird now hung from the bridge, feet dangling. His mud-caked wings were outstretched on the edge. Unable to fly, he clung on for dear life.

"Evelyn! Please help me!" 2-Tor scrambled, kicking his legs.

She had half a mind to leave him. She had warned the bird that it wasn't safe for him up here, that she didn't want to be followed, that there was no point in him sticking around. If he got hurt while chasing after her, it was his own fault.

But that was too cruel. Evie could never be so heartless. She loved the silly old bird. Turning around, she ran across the slippery stone bridge, ignoring her own safety. 2-Tor was in danger. She didn't have time to be cautious.

"Help! Heeeeelp!!!" 2-Tor was slipping. Evie grabbed his wing, but her fingers slid off with all the mud.

"2-Tor, no!" Evie wailed as the bird fell into open air. He flapped his muddy wings, trying to stay up. But the rain was too hard, and the mud too thick. He vanished into the trees far below.

Evie shrieked in horror. Now what had she done? She raced across the bridge and carefully scaled down the cliffs of Mount Luck. Gritting her teeth, Evie struggled to keep good handholds on the side of the mountain. Her hands were wet and shaking.

Several minutes later, she reached the base of the mountain. Down in the valley, rainwater surged through rivers of mud. Evie splashed down into the deepest part of the ravine.

She came to a glade she had never encountered on her many hikes through the wilderness. It was green and peaceful, surrounded by big trees. In the middle was a deep pool. A silvery substance filled the pool and had splashed across the ground in a circle. The area was littered with trash: torn-up Styrofoam cups, empty egg cartons, crumpled tin foil, and rotting Chinese takeout containers.

As Evie ventured forward, she kicked something with her foot. Pain shot through her bare toe. She crouched down to inspect the ouch-inducing object. It was a small pink mechanical bird. Its talons held the top half of a shattered plastic jar. The residue of a foul-smelling and unidentifiable substance was still inside.

"Ev- . . . Ev- . . . Evelyn . . ." chimed a strange voice from the pool. Limping on her throbbing foot, Evie ventured forward.

2-Tor's black wing stuck out of the pool and then sank beneath the surface.

Evie cried out, "2-Tor! 2-Tor! Answer me! Stupid bird!" She bit her lip, looking around frantically for something to fish him out of the silvery pool.

With a splash, 2-Tor appeared. The thick liquid dripped down his face . . . his metal face. Evie covered her mouth.

The bird turned, clacking his silver beak and staring at her with glowing red eyes. From deep within his robotic voice box, the bird-shaped machine growled, "Miss Evelyn . . . It is time for a quiz."

IT TOOK MOST OF THE DAY TO SORT THROUGH THE SMASHED REMAINS OF LANE MANSION, pulling from the twisted metal and broken furniture any mementos that were still intact. Some of Dad's equipment was salvageable, as well as old family photo albums, which had been kept in a locked safe in the master bedroom. Rick's video game systems were smashed to smithereens, adding a few new lines to the list of reasons to be mad at Evie.

Mom had been great at cleaning up the mess. Go figure. Sometimes having a parent who ran a global cleaning company had its perks. In the late afternoon, once the freak rainstorm had lifted, the Lanes finished sorting the mansion's remnants into piles: Saved, Fixable, and Junk. Rick and his parents then sat on the beach for an overdue lunch of peanut-butter-and-banana sandwiches.

"I'm worried about Evie and 2-Tor," Dad said sadly. "They should have been back by now."

Rick chewed his food and said nothing. While Dad was

correct that it was strange for Evie not to have returned—and Rick was feeling pangs of regret for lashing out at her the way he had—Rick couldn't help but be glad she was gone. Besides the destruction she caused, Evie had abandoned their mission to forge a new society. All she cared about was having fun and breaking rules. Rick had learned quickly on this continent that rules were important. They maintained order, kept people safe, and reflected the vision of the society that enforced them. That society, in Rick's case, was a place where scientists were free to pursue daring research and explore the impossible.

In the distance, out on the ocean, a cluster of ships was coming toward the continent. Rick squinted, trying to see who it was.

"Looks like transport ships," Dad said. "Newcomers."

No rest for a continent creator, Rick thought as he wolfed down the rest of his lunch in one bite and hurried back to the center of the settlement, where most of the workshops had been placed. This was the manufacturing hub, where settlers built inventions that helped the continent tick. Rick issued orders to all the workers in earshot. More immigrants were coming to the *new* new world, and soon!

The transport ships dropped anchor offshore and sent small water buses over to the beach, shuttling the new citizens of the continent to land. Every week it seemed more people arrived. It was hard to make room. They only had so many shelters, although the robots were always building more. Growth had been exponential: the population kept doubling, then doubling again. But as long as the newcomers had smarts and skills and an eagerness to build, the Lanes would make space.

The first boat arrived. Families climbed out and set their suitcases down in the sand. One group came from Zimbabwe, another from Italy, a third from Kuala Lumpur. The eighth continent was an international affair.

"Ah, salutations!" Rick hurried down the beach toward them, adjusting his glasses. "I'm Richard Lane. Call me Rick. If you head up this way, my friends will show you where to place your luggage and where you can wash up. The dining hall is at the western end of the main road—you can get a bite to eat there any time."

He felt like he was screwing up his greeting. Evie usually welcomed the new citizens, as she had a way of winning people over with just a couple of words. Her style of dancing around whatever subject she was talking about always bugged Rick, but somehow everyone else always ate it up like 2-Tor with a big bowl of worms.

"Where's the surf shop?" asked one of the kids who was wearing a Hawaiian shirt.

"There's no surf shop," Rick said sternly. "We're forming a new society, an intellectual society. We are here to do hard work."

"I heard there'd be smoothies," an old lady in the crowd complained.

"Smoothies? What are you talking about?" The confusion rose in Rick's voice.

"Isn't this New Miami?" The kid in the Hawaiian shirt seemed thoroughly unimpressed with everything.

"New Miami!?" That was a name Rick hadn't heard in a long time, and he wished it could have been longer. New Miami was the dream city of Vesuvia Piffle, a nasty tween villain who had been trying to steal the eighth continent from Rick and Evie since the very beginning. She was the super-secret CEO of the multinational real estate conglomerate the Condo Corporation, and there was no low treachery she would not stoop to if it meant winning the eighth continent all for herself. Twice the Lanes had thwarted her plans, and Rick hadn't heard anything from her or Condo Corp since stopping her at the Pacific ink stain.

"Anyone looking for New Miami has come to the wrong place. But if you're here to work for Lane Industries and form a new brilliant civilization, then raise your hand!"

About half the people in the crowd shuffled their feet and tentatively raised their hands.

"Well, fine. Anyone looking for New Miami can get back on the boats."

There was a mad dash as families raced to be first back on the boats. The water buses pulled away from shore as people splashed into the shallows, tossing their suitcases aboard before their friends pulled them in.

Rick scowled, looking over the faces of the small group that remained. "Well, at least I have you all. Now, the first thing we should do is establish each of your expertises."

Before he could continue, a blast of blaring music broke

the quiet. It sounded horrendous, like a chorus of roaring tigers underscored by a vacuum cleaner ensemble.

A sleek white speedboat was cutting a sharp wake toward the shore. Behind the wheel was a teenage boy in a purple leather trenchcoat. His silvery hair stood straight up in one big spike, and he wore round spectacles that looked like red gemstones, concealing his eyes. Strapped to his back were two enormous stereo speakers that throbbed with each pulsing beat.

The newcomers sprinted for cover as the speedboat ran aground, stopping just inches from where Rick stood. He folded his arms over his chest and gave the boy his most intolerant glare. "If you are looking for New Miami, then you have come to the wrong place."

"New Miami?" The boy leaped from the speedboat with a flourish and landed, his expensive boots kicking up two puffs of sand. He waved his hands like an orchestra conductor, and the music went silent. "Naw, man, I'm looking for that sweet settlement. The coolest of communes. The one, the only, eighth continent home of Lane Industries!"

He raised his arms, and thunderous applause erupted from his speakers. He fanned the air with his hands. Amazingly, this gesture seemed to pump up the volume.

"How are you doing that?" Rick asked inquisitively.

"Augmented reality, little dude." He wiggled his red glasses. "You should see all the sweet holograms and digital stuff these babies project onto the real world. Voice control. Gesture control. Who needs a mouse and a keyboard when

I can wield my entire electro-entertainment empire with the power of my body and mind alone?"

Rick had used augmented reality glasses before, but this boy's setup was quite sophisticated. He was like some sort of techno music magician.

"Well, we're happy to have you," Rick said. "I'm Rick Lane. I—"

"I know who you are, little dude. You think I'd come all this way without doing my homework? Tristan Ruby, cyber rock star and party planner extraordinaire, at your service." The boy extended his hand, and a swell of music came out of the speakers, as if something monumental was about to happen.

Rick reached out to shake Tristan's hand, but at the last second the boy snapped his fingers and a silver card appeared in his hand. Rick hesitated, then took the card. By just one touch Rick could tell that it was cyber paper. He squeezed the card, and it played Tristan's theme music, an overly digitized orchestral fanfare.

"I think I can help you with your public relations problem." The cocky grin on Tristan's face did not amuse Rick one bit.

"What public relations problem?"

"Your pitch, little dude! No one wants to come to a tropical paradise and do hard work. They want to relax. Hang out. No rules. Have fun! I'm a party planner. You know what that means?"

Rick glowered. "Does it mean you plan parties?"

Tristan snapped his fingers again. "Knife sharp, little dude. Knife sharp. That's exactly what it means. Let me plan a killer party for your family. I'll make the Lane settlement the coolest digs on all *ocho continentos*. We'll get celebrities, reality TV stars, pop musicians—we're talking grade-A famous people. They'll be falling over each other trying to get here once I get my nightclub set up."

"Nightclub? Whoa, whoa, *whoa*. Who said anything about a nightclub? This settlement is about science and hard work."

"Science, schmience." A deep raspy sound blatted out of Tristan's speakers, like a foghorn. "Leave it to me, little dude. I'll make the eighth continent *cool*."

A hovership roared overhead, circling the settlement. Rick shielded his eyes and squinted up at it—a Winterpole shuttle. But there was no way Winterpole could get past the protective force field Rick and his dad had built, unless . . .

"Let me think about it, Mister Ruby." Rick started back up the beach, toward where the Winterpole shuttle had landed.

As he approached, the side door of the shuttle slid open, and a girl in a three-piece suit, the standard uniform for an agent of Winterpole, stepped out. Her dark hair was pulled back in a tight bun, but two wisps curled down, framing her cheeks. She had soft brown eyes and a sweet smile that looked nothing like the other Winterpole employees Rick had met. But this was no average Winterpole employee.

"Diana!" Rick cheered and ran to her.

She sighed in relief when she saw him. "Rick! It's good to see you. Where's Evie?"

Rick groaned. "It's a long story. What's up? How goes the secret campaign to bring down Winterpole?"

"Shh!" She hushed him, her eyes darting around to see if anyone was listening or watching. "It won't be a secret if you keep talking about it so loudly. And I'm not trying to *bring them down*, I'm just doing what I can to get them to return to their original mission—unoppressively maintain order and preserve the planet's environment."

Winterpole was an eco-protection agency that had had it out for Rick's family for as long as he could remember. Diana's mother was a high-ranking officer in the organization, and she, along with many of Winterpole's top agents, like the persistent Mister Snow, kept trying new ploys to stop the Lanes from setting up their society on the eighth continent. Diana had her own agenda. She wanted to limit Winterpole's bureaucracy so it could focus on its actual mission. Unfortunately, this was no easy task. She had freed Rick's father from the Prison at the Pole when he was last arrested by Mister Snow, and since then, Diana had been the Lanes' snoop on the inside, alerting them to Winterpole's crafty plans.

"Something big is happening, Rick. I'm nervous. We should talk somewhere private."

Rick sent a quick message to his parents on his pocket tablet, alerting them to Diana's arrival. Then he took her to the *Roost*. That was the most private place he could think of.

Along the way, he explained what had happened that morning with the mansion and how Evie had stormed off into the jungle.

Diana frowned when Rick finished the story. "I hope Evie is okay. She must have felt so bad about what happened."

"She must have felt like the most irresponsible little lump on all eight continents," Rick said with a humph. "But I'm sure she'll be back soon, blaming me for everything that went wrong."

They met up with Rick's parents in the *Roost*'s navigation room. Dad made Diana a cup of raspberry iced tea, which she drank graciously. Sweets and berries were both prohibited in Winterpole facilities. Had Rick gone to visit Diana, all she would have been able to offer him was ice.

"So what's Winterpole up to now?" Rick asked as Diana drained her glass.

She wiped her mouth on the sleeve of her junior agent uniform. "I've been issued orders to deliver this to you in an official capacity. My mom thought I'd enjoy giving you the bad news myself. If only she knew how I really felt about your family . . . but never mind all that. You'd better read this."

Diana opened her shoulder bag and produced a heavy stack of white paper. Faint black type lined every page. Rick's dad picked up the papers and inspected them carefully. "Looks like some kind of cease-and-desist." He sighed and slapped the papers down on the table. "Haven't they learned that they don't get to set rules for the eighth continent? We are outside of Winterpole's jurisdiction. They have no power here."

Tucking one of her dangling curls behind her ear, Diana said, "Yes, but they do get to regulate everything that happens on the other seven continents, and that's where the trouble is. Here . . . I should just explain. You can build whatever kind of settlement you want here on the eighth continent, but Winterpole has established strict guidelines for what kind of place people from the other seven continents can move to. If a settlement, even on the eighth continent, doesn't meet Winterpole's guidelines—and there are a lot of guidelines—then people won't be able to move there."

"Well, that's a real cork on our cauldron!" Dad sounded more agitated than Rick had heard him in a long time. "This is exactly the kind of back-door obstructionism we were trying to get away from."

"Calm down, George." Mom put her comforting hands on his shoulders. "Getting worked up is no good for your heart. Winterpole wants you riled."

Dad sighed. "I know. You're right, honey."

"So what can we do?" Rick asked, flipping through the papers Diana had brought.

"You'll have to apply for a certificate of occupancy," she explained. "It's paperwork. You know how Winterpole operates. You have to meet all their guidelines for what a model settlement should be. Schools, hospitals, government buildings, infrastructure. The works. Set up everything, pass a Winterpole inspection, and the certificate is yours."

"Okay!" Rick said, getting excited. "That's not so bad. Those are all things we hope to implement in the settlement anyway. So we start work now, and in another six months or a year, we'll pass that inspection, no problem. We'll over-tax the worker robots in the meantime, but that's nothing to get stressed about."

Diana grimaced. "Uh, Rick . . . there's just one problem. The window to apply for the certificate expires in just *five days*. If you don't pass the inspection by then, you'll never be able to acquire it, and no one will be allowed to move to the eighth continent—ever."

"Five days? But that's impossible."

"Yeah!" Rick's dad added. "It's almost like Winterpole doesn't *want* us to pass the inspection."

"That's Winterpole," Diana said sadly. "In 1954, then Director of Winterpole Margot Snurslot grew tired of receiv-ing applications and other documents months after the issue dates, so she established the five-day rule. All appli-cations must be received within a five-day window of their solicitation. It's a necessity when you consider the billions and billions of requests Winterpole receives. Here's the bot-tom line: you got your continent, but Winterpole will do everything it can to keep you from forming a society here."

"Don't get down, Rick." Dad gave him a reassuring smile. "We'll think of something. We're Lanes. We always do."

Diana rose from her seat. "I'd better go. I'm going to be late getting back as it is."

"Stay," Rick said. "We'll need your help."

With a shake of her head, Diana replied, "I won't be help to anyone if Winterpole finds out what I've been up to. I'll do my best to keep you posted on whatever develops. I'm sorry I can't offer more. Goodbye, Mr. Lane, Mrs. Lane. I'm sorry, Rick. Good luck. You're going to need it."

4

A CLOUD OF GUILT HUNG OVER DIANA AS SHE PILOTED HER HOVERSHIP AWAY FROM THE LANE settlement. She felt so helpless, bringing bad news and then leaving without offering any assistance. But suspicious eyes were on her all the time. Her mother didn't trust her, Mister Snow didn't trust her, and the other junior agents were always trying to bring her down. The circumstances of George Lane's escape from the Prison at the Pole were suspicious, to say the least, and the Lane family had been especially effective at avoiding Winterpole's traps of late. It was obvious they were getting help from somewhere. Combine that with Diana's history with another Winterpole enemy, her ex–best friend Vesuvia Piffle, and it wasn't hard to see why she was feeling constricted at Winterpole Headquarters.

A loud chittering sound pulled Diana from her reverie—a sound like a cross between a cicada and a robot squirrel. But it was just the old tickertape printer the Winterpole shuttles used to communicate. Diana could guess what the message said before she even read it. She'd taken too long delivering the bad news to the Lanes. Two penalties!

Fearing the worst, she tore off the message and studied the narrow print.

```
WP—OFFICIAL COMMUNIQUE
FROM—SNOW, SRA
TO—MAPLE, JRA
REROUTE DESTINATION.
INPUT NEW COORDINATES.
OVERRIDE EXISTING OBJECTIVES.
NEW DESTINATION:
6701-Q4CX2A.
```

That's strange, Diana thought. Her existing destination coordinates were Winterpole Headquarters back in Geneva, Switzerland. These new coordinates were nowhere near there; she could tell just from looking. In fact, the new coordinates were close by. *Very* close by.

She punched the new coordinates into the navigation system. Her stomach lurched as the shuttle swung around onto its new trajectory. Diana couldn't believe it . . . the shuttle was headed back to the eighth continent.

Over the landscape the shuttle soared. It truly was a beautiful continent. She found it hard to believe that the lush forests and rolling hills had at one point been the Great Pacific Garbage Patch.

The shuttle took her to the north end of the continent,

a rocky patch of terrain crossed with natural springs and streams. Scores of Winterpole hoverships, tanks, and other machines were parked on the rocks in a neat, orderly grid. An agent in one of Winterpole's trademark iceberg helmets waved a glowing wand to direct Diana to a landing bay.

When she emerged from her shuttle, two agents, a man and a boy, were waiting for her. The man was middle-aged, smooth-cheeked, and his hair was dark, except for his white sideburns. He wore a crisp suit, white as a fresh piece of printer paper.

The suit was what made Diana's eyebrow go up. This was new. "Congratulations on your promotion, Mister Snow," she said with a slight bow.

Mister Snow straightened the bottom of his suit coat. "Your words have been recognized, Junior Agent Maple. Yes, the Director has given me command of the massive operation you see around you. This is big, very big, perhaps the largest Winterpole undertaking in twenty years."

The boy at Mister Snow's side sneered, smoothing back his greasy dark hair. "You're looking haggard and unproductive, as usual, Diana."

"Why, thank you, Benjamin," Diana retorted sarcastically. "I'm surprised that with so much time to think about it, you couldn't come up with a better insult than that."

"That's because my daily schedule blocks out only a few meager seconds to ponder the uselessness of inferior Winterpole agents."

Classic Benjamin Nagg. As good at being a vicious toad as he was at being a Winterpole junior agent. He and

Diana had started at Winterpole around the same time and studied together in the junior agent trainee program. For whatever twisted reason, he'd had it out for Diana from the very beginning. Meanwhile, the grown-ups loved everything Benjamin did, which only made it worse.

"If you two are done bickering," Mister Snow interrupted, "I will explain the purpose of our visit to this reformed garbage patch."

He guided Diana and Benjamin past complicated machinery and agents hard at work. There were slush-makers, cave-burrowing drills, paperwork-sorting devices, all sorts of things.

Mister Snow adjusted his tie as they walked. "You both well understand the unique challenge this new landmass provides. Winterpole has jurisdiction over the seven continents, but not this eighth one. There are statutes in place to keep people from moving to the Lane settlement, but that is only phase one of Winterpole's master plan. We can't legislate private settlements on the continent, but we can legislate our own. And so here we are! Welcome to the Nation of Winterpole."

"Nation of Winterpole?" Diana asked in disbelief.

"That's right! Our very own country, here on the eighth continent. Think of all the paperwork a whole country can store. Think how orderly our citizens will behave. We will uphold the ideals of our great agency, flex our bureaucratic muscles, and let our influence stretch across the entire landmass."

"It sounds like a brilliant plan," said Benjamin, sucking up.

"In the Nation of Winterpole, our statutes are once again in effect. The Director is very eager to track our progress. To make sure establishment of our new society goes smoothly, I have requested the services of Winterpole's top two junior agents."

"Who is number one, and who is number two?" Benjamin asked.

Ignoring him, Mister Snow gave Diana a stern glare. "Consider yourselves conscripted."

Benjamin looked happier than a pig at a vegan restaurant. He'd get to boss people around and torment the Lanes—his two favorite things. He immediately ran over to a squad of agents who were operating one of the snow machines and started shouting about how they were spraying snow all wrong.

Meanwhile, Diana fretted about Mister Snow's revelation. Winterpole was creating its own country on the eighth continent where they could make their own rules. And Winterpole made so, so many rules. But that wasn't the scary thing scratching at the back of Diana's mind. The Lanes created the eighth continent so they could start a new society. Winterpole had stolen that idea—quite easily, in fact. And if Winterpole was smart enough to come up with that plan, Diana worried who else would try to make their own nation on the eighth continent.

She thought she had an idea who.

EVIE SEARCHED THE GLADE IN A PANIC. THERE HAD TO BE SOME WAY TO FISH 2-TOR OUT OF THE POOL, but she was afraid to go near the silver liquid. A glob splashed the ground in front of her feet. On contact, the grass shriveled into sheets of soiled plastic. A frightful image crossed her mind of what could happen if the liquid touched her skin.

She ran to the nearest tree and broke off a low-hanging branch. It came free with a snap. Back in the pool, 2-Tor was screeching. "Help! Help! I feel so stiff. So heavy. What is happening to me?"

"2-Tor, you need to calm down! Try to stay afloat." Evie stumbled over the litter, struggling with the heavy branch. She held it over the pool. "Grab onto this, 2-Tor!"

He raised his wings out of the pool and wrapped them around the branch, pulling it under the surface. Evie strained her muscles, fighting to keep her grip and pull the bird from the pool. As she withdrew the branch, she saw it had become an old aluminum drainpipe that crunched under the strain of 2-Tor's robot wings.

Working together with Evie, 2-Tor crawled onto stable

ground. Evie dropped the branch/pipe in exhaustion and collapsed in a heap. 2-Tor lay still. The silver liquid drained off his metal shell and pooled around him, forming a bed of trash and garbage bags. The earth morphed into refuse before Evie's eyes.

"System recalibrating," 2-Tor muttered, his eyes blinking. Each piece of his metal body moved, one at a time, reestablishing connections.

"2-Tor . . ." Evie said breathlessly. "Whatever's in that pool, it looks like it's undoing whatever the Eden Compound did to you, back during the Battle of the Garbage Patch."

"Affirmative," 2-Tor chirped. "I feel my artificial intelligence coming back online. Will return to peak efficiency in . . . thirty minutes."

"I'm sorry, 2-Tor. I'm so sorry. You loved being a real bird." Evie sniffed, wiping her eyes. The list of things she had royally messed up continued to grow.

2-Tor said, "I am not programmed to feel regret, Evelyn. All is well."

Evie bit her lip, thinking about her next move. "You'll be ready to go in thirty minutes. That's, like, one episode of cartoons. We'll wait here while you power up, and then we'll head back home. Dad should take a look at you. Make sure there's no lasting damage."

If 2-Tor heard her, he made no reply. So Evie pulled his limp robot body under the shelter of a nearby tree. After a while (and it certainly seemed longer than an episode of cartoons) the rain stopped, but still 2-Tor showed no sign of recovering. At the bottom of the ravine, surrounded by trash and with nothing but 2-Tor's silent robot body for company, Evie felt truly alone. Tears crept into her eyes.

"No salt, nope!" she mumbled, wiping her face. Crying was for babies. She wasn't about to cry. But everything awful was piling up like the trash that had formed the garbage patch. It wasn't fair. Evie didn't know how things could get any worse.

The high-pitched whine of a hover engine filled the air. Evie looked to the sky for the source of the sound. For a second, she wondered if it was Rick and her parents coming to look for her. But she knew the sounds of the *Roost* and her father's hovership the *Condor* like she knew the voices of old friends. This wasn't them.

The vehicle that appeared in the air above her looked like an enormous flower, petals spinning like helicopter blades. The hovership was plastic and pink. She had seen a similar ship once before, but that flyer was not nearly so big.

Evie's stomach tightened. Her throat went dry.

A hatch opened at the bottom of the stem of the flying flower. A number of objects tumbled from the opening to the ground, forming robot-sized craters where they landed. Each object was a pink plastic robot beaver, which scurried to the edge of the glade and gnawed hungrily on the trunks of the different trees. In seconds, a large square of trees had toppled over, and the wood had been chewed to sawdust. Evie watched in disgust at the efficient and destructive way the robo-animals cleared a landing pad.

The hovership touched down, and the spinning petals slowed to a stop.

A perfectly coiffed blond head emerged from the exit hatch at the base of the stem, followed by the elegantly dressed and primly poised figure of the worst person in the world.

"Vesuvia Piffle," Evie spat, sounding like she was about to throw up. "What are you doing on my continent?"

The other ten-year-old squinted. "Peevy Evie *Lame*. Is that really you? I should have known. I felt a disturbance as my flowercopter was landing. A terrible dresser and frightful bore is close by. Beware. Beware!"

"Yeah," Evie retorted. "Beware the girl who always ruins your plans. What have you been failing miserably at lately?"

Vesuvia rubbed her temples. "Ugh, stop it, you whiskered worm. You're going to give me wrinkles."

Evie rose to her feet, glaring defiantly at her adversary. "What are you doing here anyway, Vesuvia? Aren't you tired of me ruining your plans all the time? I'll do it again. Heck, I'll do it right now."

"Oh, yeah?" Vesuvia sneered. "You and who? Your little bird brain over there?"

Behind Evie, 2-Tor was flat on his back. His robo-eyes blinked. "Warning. Hazard detected. Status: very rude."

"Yeah," Evie said awkwardly. "Me and him. I'm not afraid of your little pink chipmunks or whatever."

"My chipmunks?" Vesuvia cackled like a wicked witch.

"Oh, Peevy Evie, the Piffle Pink Patrol has had a few up-grades since you last met them."

Two massive robo-gorillas lumbered out of the flower-copter. Vesuvia leaned casually against one of the mechanical brutes, looking like a doll one of them could grasp in a fist.

"Oh, hello, my sweet monkeys," she purred. "Seize the ugly girl and her never-shut-uppy bird. Ooooh, Mommy will just love that I captured one of those losers copying our idea to start a new country on the eighth continent."

"Your idea?!" Evie fumed with rage, but before she could protest further, the robo-gorillas were charging her and 2-Tor. The robot's battery was too low to fight. Evie wasn't fast enough. And she couldn't leave 2-Tor anyway.

"Don't worry, Evie," Vesuvia soothed mockingly as the gorillas dragged her aboard the flowercopter. "Being my prisoner won't be all bad. You're going to just *love* New Miami."

VESUVIA EASED GRACEFULLY INTO THE CUSH-IONED CAPTAIN'S CHAIR OF HER FLOWERCOPTER.

Through the main viewport, a giant windshield that stretched from one end of the bridge to the other, she could watch the eighth continent pass below.

She flipped open the control panel built into her arm-rest and pushed the very big pink button, which was next to two medium-sized pink buttons and one little pink button. "Didi! I need you!" Vesuvia shrieked.

A plate slid open in the ceiling, and a basketball-sized D-2 mechanical eye came down, attached to a long robotic arm. The eye was hot pink, of course. A haughty female voice came out of the voice box on top of the eye. "My sonic sensors are quite receptive, Vesuvia. There's no reason to scream like a teakettle every time you need something. Now, how may I be of service to you?"

"Gimme a pink pineapple smoothie," Vesuvia snapped.

"*Give me* a pink pineapple smoothie, *please*," Didi replied.

"Fine! Please! Just hurry. My throat hurts, and I am so parched."

"Probably from all that shouting," Didi muttered. Seconds later, a curly plastic straw emerged from the back of Vesuvia's chair. She fed the end into her mouth and slurped graciously.

"Om . . . nom . . ."

"Will that be all, Vesuvia?"

"Sssslurrrrp! No! Footbath. Report on the latest developments at New Miami, and bring up the security feed of the main storage hold."

The robotic eye stared at Vesuvia. Then, with a hum of servos, it blinked.

Vesuvia groaned. "Fine. *Please!*"

A panel in the floor slid aside, and a bucket of steaming hot water popped up. Vesuvia kicked off her pleather shoes and dipped her feet in the water. She had such a chill from going out after the rain.

Didi rattled off facts and figures about the latest progress in the construction of New Miami. Normally this stuff bored the fluff out of Vesuvia, but when it came to New Miami, nothing was more important.

Vesuvia liked having her own artificial intelligence, or AI. Mastercorp had given her the robotic assistant when she took the job at her mother's urging. But sometimes Didi was so rude! She sounded like all those witchy teachers at school who told Vesuvia she wasn't good for anything because she never applied herself. All Vesuvia wanted was a best friend who always complimented her and did whatever she commanded. Was that so much to ask? She had added some modifications to Didi's programming when she first acquired her. It had helped—now Didi had impeccable taste in clothes and a large catalogue of the coolest pop music—but sometimes she teased Vesuvia mercilessly for not knowing some high-tech mumbo jumbo, and she never did Vesuvia's homework for her, the way Diana had.

When Didi finished her report, she brought up the security camera Vesuvia had requested on the main viewscreen. The main storage hold was a dark chamber at the base of the flowercopter. In the dim light, Vesuvia could just make out Evie struggling against her jailers. The two hulking robo-gorillas held her by her wrists and ankles, restraining her completely. Evie tried to worm her way free, grunting in pain and discomfort. But it was no use.

"Make sure my monkeys are holding her tight!" Vesuvia said.

"Tightly," Didi corrected. "And gorillas are apes, not monkeys."

Vesuvia hissed at the robot eye. "Stop correcting me!"

Before she could yell at Didi further, the AI said, "Beginning our approach to New Miami."

Squealing with joy, Vesuvia switched off the security camera feed and ran to the viewscreen, slipping and splashing footbath water across the bridge. In the distance she could see it—her perfect pink jewel. Construction had begun a month earlier, and progress had been steady. Vesuvia had found a narrow peninsula that ran along the west coast of the continent. It was a sandy stretch of land, but it served her need for lots of beachfront property perfectly. The Piffle Pink Patrol had built docks and construction yards. Condo Corp had brought in hotels, restaurants, and shopping malls. Mastercorp provided security. Rich tourists had already arrived, paying top dollar to be among the first visitors to the ultimate vacation destination.

The flowercopter landed on the roof of the Pink Palace, Vesuvia's luxury hotel at the southern tip of New Miami Beach. As Vesuvia fastened her shoes back on, getting ready to leave, Didi said, "Mastercorp dreadnought approaching. Viola Piffle requests an immediate audience."

Vesuvia sighed. Her mother was always showing up with those Mastercorp goons at the worst times. Why couldn't they leave her alone to work on building New Miami?

"Fine," she said, annoyed. "Hold our guests here until I come back. Blech. Why does everything have to be so difficult?"

"At least you can walk around," Didi said mournfully. "I'm stuck on this flowercopter."

"That must really stink for you," Vesuvia said, turning up her nose. "Good thing I don't care about your problems at all."

Vesuvia went inside the hotel and took the super-speed

elevator down to the bottom floor. She pushed out the front doors and crossed the parking lot to the edge of Condo Cove. The Mastercorp dreadnought was pulling up to the dock. The massive submarine was the shape of a black shark. It was so huge the vessel could easily swallow the Pink Palace whole.

The shark opened its mouth as it approached the dock, and an entry ramp emerged from the gaping maw like a long, serpentine tongue. Vesuvia crossed the ramp and entered the dreadnought.

There was never enough light inside the Mastercorp vessel. It gave Vesuvia the distinct sensation of being trapped inside the belly of a real shark. Yuckfest. As she reached the dock inside the shark's mouth, she spotted Mister Dark waiting for her. The Mastercorp officer was creeptastic—that was the nicest thing Vesuvia could say about him. He was weird and intimidating, but she couldn't really explain why. He gave her a general sense of unease, but whenever she tried to visualize him in her mind, no image appeared. He was simply the black suit. The details of his hair and face weren't there, as if someone had airbrushed them out of her mind.

"Follow me, Piffle." It wasn't a request. Mister Dark led Vesuvia through the dank hallways of the dreadnought, at last arriving in a big research laboratory near the heart of the ship.

Vesuvia's mother stood at the far side of the lab, examining the molecular composition of strange chemical compounds on a big holo-display. Vesuvia rolled her eyes. All this nerd stuff was so boring.

"Hello, Vesuvia," her mother said. "We expected you sooner."

"Oh, Mummy, I have the most delicious news! I have captured that ugly weasel, Evie Lane."

"Truly?" Viola Piffle was an intense woman, tall and fair with hair like platinum. Humorless and merciless, she always seemed in control. She turned to look at her daughter, a thin eyebrow raised.

Vesuvia wondered if that expression meant her mother was pleased. "Yes. And her stinking talking bird too. They're back at the Pink Palace right now."

Viola exchanged a quiet glance with Mister Dark. "One of the Lane children in our grasp? Well, this is good news."

"And that's not all, Mummy. Can you believe the stupid bird got turned back into a robot?"

"What?" her mother snapped, swooping close to her daughter and grabbing her by the shirt. It was the first time her mother had touched her since she had reappeared months earlier, working for Mastercorp. "The bird changed back? The same bird that was exposed to the Eden Compound and turned into a real bird?"

"Ack! Don't wrinkle my blouse." Vesuvia squirmed. "Yes, the same bird. I guess so. Who cares?"

"How did this happen?" Viola tightened her grip. "Tell me!"

"Ow! That hurts!" Vesuvia wrestled free. "I don't know!"

Viola snapped at Mister Dark, "Bring the girl and the bird aboard the dreadnought immediately. We'll hold them prisoner here. There are tests I'll need to conduct."

Without a word, Mister Dark left the room, disappearing like a shadow exposed to light.

"But Mummy!" Vesuvia pouted. "I had such nasty things planned for Evie."

"Our work is infinitely more important than your petty revenge. Besides, I'm sending you on a mission."

"Yuck! I hate missions! I want to keep working on New Miami."

Viola gave her daughter a disgusted look. "You sound like your father when you whine like that. Don't act so pathetic."

Vesuvia seethed but remained silent.

"Mastercorp just received word that Winterpole has issued new immigration restrictions on anyone attempting to move to the eighth continent. The Lanes will be trying to build up their settlement so they can acquire a certificate of occupancy. Do you know what that means?"

"Do I look like I care?" Vesuvia asked.

"No! You don't. And that's why you're such a stupid girl. If the Lanes get that certificate, they'll be able to build on the continent. But that can't happen. Mastercorp needs to rid this continent of the Lane blight so we can maximize the sprawl of our factories and weapons testing grounds. Your mission is to smash everything the Lanes have built so that they never get their certificate."

"Okay." Vesuvia smiled. "That sounds like oodles of fun."

"It's not supposed to be fun. Quit being such a good-for-nothing layabout and do your job. Then come back. Once the Lane settlement has been destroyed and *we* acquire the certificate of occupancy, we will have much more of the eighth continent for Mastercorp."

"And I'll be able to expand New Miami clear across the continent," Vesuvia added.

Viola turned away, as if she had concluded the conversation was over. "You are wasting time, daughter. Get going."

EVIE WOKE WITH A SHIVER.
SHE WAS LYING ON A CONCRETE SLAB IN AN

utterly blank room. The walls were smooth, stained with years of mildew and who knew what else. Her only vantage out of the room was through the metal bars covering one wall of her cell. Beyond the bars was a dark, narrow hallway.

The previous night began to come back to her as she wiped the crust of dry tears from her eyes. Separated from 2-Tor, she was dragged aboard the enormous black robo-shark and flung into this box. The gorillas had not been gentle.

As she sat up on the slab, she massaged her bruised arm and shook her head in dismay. New Miami, on *her* continent. Beautiful grassy fields had been chewed up into rough dirt, where condominiums and boutiques were installed. The trees, those beautiful young trees Sprout and Professor Doran had created—there was no telling where they had gone. Killed by the saws of Vesuvia's robots, most likely. What hurt the most about all the *development* was that there had been so many people hanging out in New Miami. New arrivals. Settlers just like those who had joined Evie's family in the place they had made. They looked like they were having so much fun. Young and old, rich and poor. How could they enjoy Vesuvia's vapid, tyrannical pleasure palace? Little Miss Perfect Piffle would pay for tampering with the natural landscape Evie and Rick had worked so hard to create.

Rick. Thinking about him hurt more than the bruises. She wished she had never run off. If she'd stayed, none of this would have happened. 2-Tor wouldn't be . . .

She shut her eyes, feeling the tears creep back.

No way was Evie going to let Vesuvia and Mastercorp toy with her one second longer. She got up, dusted herself off, and went to the bars of her cell. There weren't any guards in the hallway, and she was a skinny kid. Turning sideways, Evie tried to squeeze through the bars. Her shoulder fit fine, but then her head got snagged.

She could almost fit, but not quite. She looked around her cell for ideas and noticed something. A tray of food rested on the floor at the foot of her bed. Well, it was sort of food. A few crusts of stale bread, a jar of strawberry jelly, and a pink plastic spoon. Her stomach grumbled, yet she couldn't bring herself to eat anything Vesuvia had provided.

But maybe she could put the food to good use.

Evie unscrewed the petite jar of jelly and stuck two fingers in it, scooping out a big glob of the smelly stuff. She felt the slippery texture. There was a chance. Her whole hand plunged into the jar and pulled out the contents, then, taking a deep breath, Evie smeared it all over her head.

Back at the cell bars, she squeezed between them, straining her head against the metal. "Come on, pull!" she muttered to herself. Rick was always calling her "pudding head." Surely a big head of pudding covered in strawberry jelly could squeeze through jail cell bars.

Evie took a deep breath, winced, and pulled.

On the other side of the bars, she tumbled to the floor. Her head felt like it had been through the washing machine—permanent press cycle—and it took a minute to make the dizziness go away. When the world returned to its proper orientation, Evie stumbled to her feet, wiped her face off on her shirt, and dashed down the hall, out of the cell block.

She emerged into a maze of corridors without a clue where she was or where to go. "Wild guess!" she blurted out and ran left.

After several hundred feet, she froze and pressed against the wall, trying to conceal herself. In the distance she could hear the percussion of combat boots on the metal floor. Seconds later, Mastercorp guards crossed the hall at the next intersection. They were running a military drill, grunting and barking orders to one another. Each soldier clutched a black assault rifle. There was nothing cute or charming about these weapons, nothing like the technology Evie's father had created or the kind that Winterpole used. These guns were for just one thing—efficient murder.

Thinking quickly, Evie slipped across the hall and into the first door that caught her eye.

The crash and clang of heavy metal weapons filled the room beyond the door. Evie dove out of the way as a robotic foot the size of an SUV stomped the ground beside her. She backed up, trying to fit the massive moving objects in her vision.

Two enormous robots sparred, a clash of the titanium titans. The machines were roughly humanoid in shape, with broad shoulders and heads like football helmets. One wielded an enormous shining sword, the other a massive battle axe. Evie's ears throbbed every time the weapons collided.

She looked around for the exit and found it, a small platform with a door leading out, ten stories up—about eye level with the battling robots.

"Good technique, Robo-One," said a business professional voice over the loudspeaker. "Let's attempt Robo-Two's disarm next."

While Evie tried to figure out what the guy on the loudspeaker was talking about, the two robots swung at each other again. The battle axe robot parried, knocking the sword out of the other robot's hand. Evie covered her head as the sword slammed into the floor beside her, knocking her off her feet.

Realizing she wasn't going to get another chance, Evie

took a deep breath and ran *toward* the fallen sword. She jumped on the flat part of the blade and held on to the hilt. The first robot picked up the weapon and hoisted the giant sword into the air, and Evie along with it. She swung wildly as she tried not to fall off. She was so small compared to the size of these robots that they didn't seem to notice her. The robot raised the sword at its opponent. Evie sprinted across the length of the outstretched blade. As she neared the tip, she leaped. Below, the weapons crashed together again, causing a shower of sparks. Evie slammed hard into the handle of the battle axe and slid down to the second robot's clenched hand. Hugging its fingers tightly, she screamed in fright as the robot raised the axe. But her plan had worked. Evie jumped from the robot to the platform, ten stories up, and ran through the door before anyone spotted her.

She barely registered the word on the sign above the door.

ANIARMAMENT.

The door slammed shut behind her. Inside, she winced at the sounds that filled the darkness. There was a clack and clatter snapping over a hiss that nearly deafened her. Machines. It was the sound of angry machines.

Large robotic structures filled the room, so tightly packed with their appendages entangled that they reminded Evie of the dense jungle surrounding New Boca, that crazy retirement community in the rainforest that Vesuvia's grandmother had built. The robots were building other robots—a kind of twisted assembly line. Dark clouds roiled in Evie's stomach.

In the center of the chaos were hundreds of robot animals, but not the kind in the Piffle Pink Patrol she had seen Vesuvia command. These were devilish creations, with accentuated fangs and knife-like claws. The grotesque faces sent a chill through her.

A flash of brown caught Evie's eye. A hand? And then a flash of pink. A foot? She looked closer, even though a voice in her head was screaming for her to look away, to shut her eyes. Were there people in these machines? Maybe it was just a trick of the light. They did not move and made no sound.

With a loud slap, a cold hand clamped down on Evie's shoulder. She screamed, but the sound was swallowed by the roar of the machines.

Mister Dark loomed over her. "What are you doing out of your cage, little bird?"

UNDER THE COVER OF DARKNESS, THE PIFFLE PINK PATROL APPROACHED THE LANE SETTLEMENT.

Vesuvia watched from inside the head of Geri, her titanic robot giraffe. Didi dangled from her eyestalk beside Vesuvia's head.

Outside the viewport, it was quiet. The treetops were still. She couldn't make out the drab, poorly arranged shelters those undignified Lanes were huddling in, but according to Didi, they were there, just beyond the line of trees.

"Forward!" Vesuvia shouted. Geri raised one of her front legs, big as a telephone pole, and marched into the forest.

Bzzzt!

The electrical charge surged through Geri, jolting Vesuvia and making her hair stand on end. Didi spun wildly in a circle.

"What in the name of sweet shopping was that?"

"Electromagnetic pulse detected. Auxiliary power systems enabled."

"Speak *English*, Didi!"

"That *was* English. Read a book, you bratty pumpkin."

"Pumpkin?! I'll rewire you into a hair dryer!" Vesuvia dove at the robotic eye.

Didi rose above Vesuvia's head, out of reach.

"Your impotent threats mean nothing to me, Vesuvia."

Growling under her breath, Vesuvia rushed to the controls and flung them forward. "Full speed ahead!"

Didi sounded frantic. "Vesuvia, no, wait!"

Geri took another step, and an even bigger surge of electrical energy rattled the robot giraffe. The viewscreen went blank. The control console powered down. The overhead lights switched off, plunging the cockpit into darkness.

"Hey! Who turned off the lights?" Vesuvia tripped and tumbled to the floor with a clang.

After a few seconds, the light in Didi's eye flickered back on. "You did," she explained, her voice low and slow before it wound back up to its normal tempo. "The Lanes have installed a force field around the perimeter of their settlement. Any attempts to pass technology through the field will result in a complete system shutdown."

"*Any* technology?" Vesuvia asked in disbelief. "Even my robo-birds? Even my pocket tablet?"

"Anything," Didi said. She took control of Geri and maneuvered away from the edge of the force field. The rest of the Piffle Pink Patrol followed.

"So how do we get in?" Vesuvia asked. She wasn't used to such setbacks. Not being able to smash the entire Lane settlement into tiny little pieces made her brain feel like a hot tub with the bubbles and heat cranked all the way up.

"Scanning . . ." The lights in Geri's head turned back on, and the control console powered up. "Connection established. Would you like to disable the EMP shield?"

"What do you think?" Vesuvia snapped. "Of course I would!" With the shield in place, any attempt to enter the Lane settlement would cause all her pretty pink robots to short circuit.

Apathetically, Didi replied, "Access denied. Password verification required."

Password. Vesuvia didn't like the sound of that. "Didi, quick, hack their system. I want to smash them! Hurry!"

"Decryption enabled." The light in Didi's eye blinked on and off rapidly, the way some computers do when they're thinking very hard. "I'm sorry, Vesuvia, but the security of this system is beyond my capacity. We will have to find the password some other way."

"So it's impossible then! Hopeless!"

Didi groaned. "You, my dear, whine more than the jet engine I used to date. I've never seen a human be so quick to quit."

"Well, what's the solution, then?"

"I'm sure you can figure it out if you give it some thought."

Vesuvia hated the way Didi was always playing games with her, like she was trying to teach her something. Vesuvia hated school. She hated learning. She hated thinking, unless it was about what to eat or what to wear. So Didi's attempts to educate Vesuvia were super annoying.

But the AI was right about one thing. Complaining wasn't going to get them through the force field. Whining wouldn't smash the Lane settlement. How could she get through?

At Condo Corp, passwords were closely guarded secrets. Only the highest-level officials were told secret codes. Most of those officials were members of Vesuvia's own family. So it stood to reason that those loser Lanes might do the same. That meant the only people with the password would be the ugly parents, that nerdy boy Rick, and—

Ew. Double ew. Vesuvia scrunched up her face in disgust.

Didi purred, "My optical sensors detect displeasure, but also a positive realization. Would you like to share, Vesuvia?"

Vesuvia did *not* want to share, but she didn't see any other option. "Evie Lane knows the password. I'm sure of it."

"Wonderful! She's in a holding cell back at the Mastercorp dreadnought. How will you get her to reveal the password to you?"

Shuddering at the thought, Vesuvia said, "I'm going to have to be nice to her."

9

PROFESSOR DORAN'S BANANA BOAT RAN AGROUND JUST AFTER DAYBREAK. RICK RACED DOWN TO THE beach to greet the new arrivals. A squad of six-foot-tall orange robots, the carrying carrots, disembarked with big bags of seeds over their tops. They marched up to the main road where Rick's parents were waiting.

Rick hopped from foot to foot, barely able to contain his excitement. It felt like the release party of the biggest video game of the year. All the anticipation was making him dizzy. For a moment, he was able to push the thoughts of worry from his mind, about the certificate of occupancy and about Evie. She still had not returned. Concern among the group had risen, and despite everything, he hoped she was safe.

A boy leaped off the front of the boat and planted his cowboy boots in the sand. The boy stood before Rick with a huge smile on his face. He wore a denim shirt and chaps over his jeans. His hat was still way too big, and his chili pepper–shaped slide gleamed in the morning light. A shiny new machete hung from a loop on his belt.

"Well, shoot, Rick!" The boy sauntered over to him, grinning wider. "You're looking finer than a turnip in a tuxedo."

Rick returned the smile joyfully. "Sprout! You made it!"

"I reckon we sure did. Took us about as long as the prof and I could imagine. Had to set sail from the Gulf of Mexico, and then we got stuck in traffic in the Panama Canal. But boy, am I excited to finally be here! Hoo-wee! Look at everything you got set up."

Rick had told Sprout so many of his dreams about what the eighth continent would be. "This is just the beginning, Sprout. You're going to help us reach the next step."

"Boy, I can't wait! Where's Evie? I gotta give her a howdy-doo."

Rick grimaced. "It's a long story."

"Long story? Well, I got time."

"Come on, Sprout. Let me show you around. Then I'll explain everything."

By the time Rick completed his tour, Sprout was giddy with excitement. There were so many possibilities! So much to do. Rick had hoped Sprout would love the eighth continent as much as he did.

The boys reconnected with Rick's parents over by his father's laboratory. They stood out front with Sprout's mentor and guardian, Professor Doran, who had also arrived on the banana boat. The professor was an old college friend of Rick's parents, though Professor Doran always seemed so stern and unimpressed with George Lane's many accomplishments. Rick could only hope that enlisting Doran's help to complete the requirements to receive the certificate of occupancy from Winterpole was the right idea.

"It won't be easy," Professor Doran said. "But there's a chance. We need to begin construction right away if we hope to finish all these buildings in time."

"How do we get started?" asked Rick's mom.

"Well, perhaps a practical demonstration is in order," said Professor Doran. "Sanchez, do you have the sample?"

"I sure do, Prof." Sprout handed over a large seed. Professor Doran squatted down, dug a little hole out of the dirt road, and buried the seed inside. Then he produced a spray bottle from his satchel, which was made of woven plant fibers.

"This is a special nutrient serum I use to accelerate plant growth. I infused the plants that created the foliage on the continent with the same mixture."

Rick watched intently as the professor sprayed the mound of dirt that covered the seed.

"Now stand back," the professor urged. "Quick. Move."

In seconds, little stems emerged from the dirt and started to stretch, spreading into leaves and vines. A wooden trunk appeared, and it kept growing wider and taller until a tree formed—more of an oversized stump, really, with only a couple of branches jutting off. When the sudden growth stopped, the plant was the size of an out-house. But the peculiar thing about the plant was that the tree was completely hollow. There were openings too, which looked a bit like round windows and doorways.

"Wow!" Sprout hooted, circling the trunk to inspect the tree. "It grew like magic."

"Not magic, my dear boy," corrected the professor. "Science."

Rick adjusted his glasses, then reached in and touched the bark of the tree. It was rough like concrete and sturdy like steel. He began to see the possibilities.

"This is called a hollow tree. It's an arboreal hybrid of my own design. These should serve our purposes just fine." The professor rubbed the bark of the tree like he was pat-ting a loyal horse.

Rick smiled. "We can build inside the trees. These can be our buildings—our laboratories and our schools."

"Precisely, my dear boy," said the professor. "I have enough seeds to create a small city. The problem is the spray. We have to be careful with how much we use. Not enough, and you get little lumpy buildings like this one. Too much, and there's no telling how big the buildings will get."

"Bigger is better," Rick said.

"Not if a tree grows so big it crashes into the other ones. That would set us back." When Professor Doran said this, Sprout's eyes grew wide.

"Good point." Rick nodded.

"And my supply of spray is limited. We have to be very careful. If we squander what we have, we may not be able to finish."

"But this is good," Rick said. "We'll be like Swiss Family Robinson, living in tree houses."

"Yeehaw!" Sprout cheered. "Sounds like fun."

Professor Doran said, "Well, if you want your fun you'd better get started. We don't have much time to complete our task."

"You don't need to tell us three times," Rick replied. "Come on, Sprout. Let's go plant some skyscrapers."

They worked until nightfall, mapping out where the trees would go and excavating holes deep enough to give a head start to the vast root systems the hollow trees required. Rick and Professor Doran calculated to the milliliter how much spray was needed to make the trees grow just right. The speed at which the trees grew had made Rick think the work would be easy, when the reality was much more laborious. Still, the speed with which the large wooden structures burst from the ground fueled their progress. At last the group collapsed, drenched with sweat and aching sore muscles, into comfortable chairs in the dining hall. The building vaguely resembled a school cafeteria, with long tables and lots of seats.

Rick was thrilled with how the settlement was coming

together. It reminded him of that first day, when the Eden Compound had fallen onto the Great Pacific Garbage Patch, and the eighth continent had formed all at once.

As the others drifted happily to a hot shower or a hot meal, Rick surveyed the work they had done and was proud. After just one day, he could already see progress. The research laboratory dominated the center of the village. The northern curve was lined with the skyscraper dormitories. Down by the beach was the welcome center and the security station. From afar, the settlement looked like a grove of tall, barren trees, some like enormous fallen logs. Soon their settlement would become a town, the town would become a city, and then . . . who knew? There was no telling how big Rick's country would grow.

He was glad to be able to share it with a dear friend like Sprout. The boy had tackled the challenge of planting the tree-buildings with his usual enthusiasm. Over dinner, Sprout told Rick about the adventures he had been on since their last encounter. He had traveled all over: Madagascar, Thailand, Sumatra. He had even conducted detailed investigations into edible cacti in various deserts around the world. Sprout's wild and hilarious stories made Rick's stomach sore from laughter.

As the boys finished their meal, Rick's parents entered the dining hall, their faces filled with concern.

"Still no word from 2-Tor or your sister," Rick's father explained. "Have either of you seen them?"

Rick shook his head.

"This is getting serious," Mom said. "We've sent out search parties to look for them—some of the workers have volunteered. We're going to start looking too."

"How can we help?" Sprout asked eagerly.

"I'd suggest you both get some rest," Dad replied. "We'll find Evie and 2-Tor. You can continue building tomorrow. Stay focused. We only have four days left to get the certificate of occupancy."

Sprout nodded, but Rick could tell from his expression that he was still worried about Evie.

Once Mom and Dad left, Sprout turned to Rick with an expression he'd never seen before, a mix of hurt and frustration.

"Why didn't you tell me she was missing, Rick? This is serious!"

"I know. I'm sorry." Rick grumbled, frustrated with himself. "I didn't know how to bring it up—and I didn't realize it was so serious. You know as well as anyone how she always goes off on her own to prove a stupid point."

"But things are different this time. Dang it, Rick. We should have been looking for her."

"But we have to finish building so we can get the certificate!"

Sprout glared. "Which is more important, this here settlement or your own gosh darn sister?"

Rick frowned and said nothing. Evie always went her own way, against the wishes and plans of the rest of the family. Rick was the one doing all the hard work. He felt used, like Evie was taking advantage of his labor. It frustrated him that he didn't know how to control her.

Sprout slapped the table. "Y'all are always acting like a two-headed dog chasing its tail. I don't see why you're always fighting all the time."

"She never listens to me, Sprout. I'm the one who has the plan. Evie even asks me what the plan should be, but then when I tell her, she argues. *You* don't do that. You just go along with the plan."

"Well, shoot, Rick, that's because I don't stand a chance of arguing with that big old brain of yours. But Evie ain't never gonna let you get away with bossing people around. She's gonna fight you every step of the way. What you don't realize is that you're better for it."

"Better?"

"Well, sure! How would you ever know if your plans are good if Evie weren't there to pick 'em apart? See, you gotta treat that girl like asparagus."

Rick tried to grin. "I have to spread Evie around on my plate so Mom thinks I ate more than I actually did?"

Sprout's eyes went wide. "First of all, why in the name of the Jolly Green Giant would you do that? Asparagus is delicious. And second, no! You have to let her grow wild, Rick. Some plants need to be kept in their special spots, tended to, micromanaged, like tomatoes. But that ain't Evie, no sir. Some plants, you wanna just throw seeds around. You never know what'll grow! How big your crop will be. That's what Evie's like. You gotta let her be wild."

Reaching out, Rick clapped Sprout on the arm and gave him a little shake. "Thanks, Sprout. I'm glad you're here. You've given me a lot to think about."

"Well, shoot, I just want my amigos to get along, if it ain't too much trouble."

Before Rick could reply, loud music started pumping from outside the dining hall. He had to cover his ears. This was not okay. Many of the little children had already gone to sleep—Rick's own bedtime was coming up. It was much too late for such loud music. It was a public disturbance to the settlement.

"Come on," Rick said, rising from his seat. "Let's go check that out."

Sprout pushed himself to his feet. "Hoo-wee! We're gonna put down that disturbance real good."

They raced out of the dining hall and onto the main road. They could see, even from this distance, the flashing lights and dancing strobes of a party in full swing in the middle of the town square. A bunch of workers and their kids were crowded around, dancing and singing along to the pumping music.

To no surprise of Rick's, Tristan Ruby stood in the middle of it all, surrounded by laser-light projections of audio sliders, turntables, a keyboard, and a floating vi-olin. His speaker-backpack was the source of the noise. Tristan's glasses flashed in the strobe light as he turned to Rick. "What's up, little dude? You look like you need to cut loose."

"I do *not* need to cut loose," Rick assured him. "I need you to turn this music off. Party's over."

Tristan grinned. He always gave off a vibe that he was only half listening. "Naw. The music's gotta stay on. Look how much fun everyone's having. I'm telling you, these cats are gonna text their friends and be like, 'Yo! The Patch is the happeningest place on all eight continents.' And then they'll come here. You'll get more people."

"The Patch?" Sprout asked.

"Yeah, you know, like 'garbage patch'? It's my new name for this place."

"Listen," Rick said, "I appreciate that you're trying to help, but this isn't how we do things around here."

"Yeah, but you ain't the boss of me, little dude. So why don't you back off?"

Rick stepped forward. "Hey, don't—"

Tristan Ruby cranked up the music. It was so loud it literally knocked Rick and Sprout off their feet. They tumbled to the ground, covering their ears in pain. But the dancers seemed to love it. They kept shaking their hips and stomping their feet, enjoying the ability to party after a hard day's work.

As Rick and Sprout stumbled back to their sleep shelters, searching fruitlessly for earplugs, Rick felt a painful longing for Evie to return. He could manage the settlement fine, just not the people in it. For that, he needed his sister.

10

"THAT'S THE LAST OF THEM," SAID THE MASTER-CORP LABORER AS HE STEPPED BACK TO ADMIRE his handiwork. The new bars of Evie's cell were much closer together. She could barely reach her arm between them. Now there was no way to escape.

As the laborer departed, Mister Dark's words still rang through her head. "The only reason I don't end your little life right now is that Mrs. Piffle sees value in you. I suggest you pray that you retain that value, but the truth is, I always get what I want in the end."

Alone now, Evie was glad there was no one to see her cry.

Whether minutes or hours passed, she wasn't sure, but Evie was still wiping her cheeks when she heard footsteps coming down the hall. She held her breath. It didn't matter who was coming to see her, she knew she wouldn't like it.

She was right. Vesuvia appeared, smiling like a beauty queen — that strained, good-grief-why-do-I-have-to-grin-like-an-idiot smile. She knocked on the bars of Evie's cell and waved when the other girl looked up.

"Hello, Evie. It's nice to see you. You're looking . . ." Half her face twisted up like she was in pain. "Fabulous. As usual."

Evie shook her head and wiped her face dry. "Oh, yeah? You look like a rodeo clown with a bad case of indigestion."

For a second, Vesuvia glared her nasty glare, but then she shook it off. "Oh, Evie, you are a *riot*. You say the funniest things. Tee hee hee."

Angrily, Evie pushed up from her slab and stomped over to the bars. "What do you want? Where's 2-Tor? Why am I here? Answer me, you . . . you . . . you continent thief!"

"Thief? That is not the spirit of sharing I would expect from the kind and generous Evelyn Lane. You know, Evie, I was just passing by the kitchens—did you know the Mastercorp dreadnought has an entire room devoted to cupcake icing? Well, I thought about bringing you a whole gallon jug of vanilla icing, but then I thought—no. Evie deserves better. And so I brought you this, the perfect breakfast for beautiful princesses everywhere."

She held out her hand. Sitting in her palm, inches from the bars of the cell, was the most perfect, scrumptious cupcake Evie had ever seen. Pink icing, a tiny sliver of strawberry poised at the peak, a vanilla base, and the paper had been replaced by a thin tuile of chocolate chip cookie. Evie licked her lips. She hadn't eaten anything since dinner the night before she left her family's settlement.

"Go on," Vesuvia said. "I brought it for you."

Slowly, Evie reached through the bars and took the

cupcake from Vesuvia's open hand like she was picking a flower. She held it in front of her face, smelling the sweet scents of sugar and strawberries. Her eyes never left Vesuvia's. The other girl, with her sparkling eyes and rosy cheeks, looked the opposite of how Evie felt—like nothing in the whole world could go wrong.

Evie flashed a grin . . . and then stuffed the cupcake in Vesuvia's face. The icing smeared her makeup. The little bit of strawberry went up her nose. She pulled away in disgust, spitting cupcake and wiping icing out of her eyes, and the rest of the confection crumbled to the floor.

"Oh, Evie, you always were a funny one." Vesuvia tried to laugh, but Evie could see the anger boiling inside of her. She pulled out her compact and inspected the deformed state of her makeup. She did her best to smooth out the smudges and touch up what she had wiped away. When she turned back to Evie, she was perfect, pristine Vesuvia again.

"Let me out of here," said Evie, deadly serious. "And where is 2-Tor?"

"Certainly!" Vesuvia said, feigning a smile. She produced an access key card from a pocket in her dress. "It's the least I can do, after you freed me from prison the same way. And as for your bird, I'll take you to him right away, of course."

True to her word, Vesuvia swiped the card, and the bars of Evie's cell swung open. She had half a mind to sock Vesuvia and make a run for it right there, but Evie knew that if that happened, the façade of niceness would evaporate.

Mastercorp agents would come flying out of the ventilation ducts or materialize out of thin air, or some other terrifying thing Evie could cook up in her subconscious. Escape would not be easy. Rather than get shoved right back into her cell by impolite robots or well-armed soldiers, she decided to play along, for now.

"Lead the way, Vesuvia," Evie said, faking a gracious bow.

A short walk through dark hallways brought them to a research laboratory. This was nothing like Evie's father's labs. Everything was clean and organized. Young scientists with trendy haircuts and bleached lab coats moved from station to station, examining samples, assessing data, and adjusting hip glasses everywhere. Rick would have been in heaven.

In the center of the room was a gyroscopic harness suspended from two large metal legs. 2-Tor was strapped into the contraption, but she barely recognized him. His feathers were gone, as was the twinkle in his eyes. He now looked as he had in the years prior to the Battle of the Garbage Patch. 2-Tor was a robot again. How had it happened? It looked like the Mastercorp scientists were trying to find out. One machine scraped off filings from his metal breast. Another sprayed him with strange liquids.

From a dais at the other end of the lab, two grown-ups watched the examination. One was a woman with sharply cut blond hair. She had the body of an Olympic athlete and the stern face of an Olympic judge. The other was a man, and although he was standing in plain sight, Evie couldn't make out his face.

When 2-Tor saw the two girls enter the lab, he shook in his harness and squawked, "Evelyn! Oh, my, you are a sight for sore optical sensors. Are you all right?"

Evie rubbed her arm. "I'm fine, 2-Tor. What have they done to you?"

"Nobody knows!" 2-Tor said. "It appears that I have undergone a retro-transformation. I'm back to my old self again—although I don't know what happened to those worms I ate yesterday for breakfast."

"Have they hurt you?" Evie asked, concerned.

"Quite the contrary, miss, these Mastercorp gentlepeople have been quite kind. I had an oil bath and a polish. They carefully examined my circuits—every wire was secured! I'm fit as an electric guitar now."

"That's great, 2-Tor, but *why* are they being so nice to you?"

"Oh!" Robot 2-Tor could not blush, but Evie thought she saw his eyes glow a little redder. "I hadn't considered it, honestly."

Evie had an idea. During the Battle of the Garbage Patch, the Eden Compound had rained on 2-Tor, turning him from a robot into a real-live seven-foot-tall talking bird. Whatever 2-Tor had fallen into back in the glade must have reverted him to his robot form. That's why all that garbage was surrounding the pool of silvery liquid! That liquid was turning whatever it touched back into what it was before it had been sprayed with the Eden Compound.

Sighing heavily, Evie turned away from 2-Tor. If Rick had been there, he would have figured out all this stuff in an instant. He would have told Evie what it all meant and what they had to do to stop anything bad from happening. But Rick wasn't here, and all this weird chemistry stuff was making Evie's head hurt.

"Over here, Evie!" Vesuvia said, skipping across the lab and up the steps to the raised platform. The two grown-ups watched Evie as she followed. "This is Mister Dark. He's a big shot at Mastercorp. And this is my beautiful mother, the glorious, illustrious, isn't-it-obvious-she-produced-such-stellar-offspring Viola Piffle!"

"What do you know about the Anti-Eden Compound?" Vesuvia's mother bent at the waist so she could look Evie more directly in the eye.

"Never heard of it," Evie said. Her heart was pounding, but she tried to remain still and not look fearful.

Mister Dark placed that cold hand on Evie's shoulder again, reminding her of their encounter in the Aniarmament room. It felt like an iron vise. "What is the chemical formula of the Eden Compound?"

Evie pulled away, terrified. "That formula was lost along with Doctor Evan Grant. *No one* has it anymore."

Vesuvia took Evie by the arms and pulled her away from Mister Dark and her mother. "You two are being very rude to my friend. She has just gotten out of her cell, you know."

This was even scarier than the intimidating Mister Dark. Her *friend*? Why was Vesuvia being so nice?

"What is going on here?" Evie asked. "What do you all want with us?"

Her eyes cold, Viola glanced at her daughter. "Tell her the deal, Vesuvia."

The little blond princess clapped her hands together. "Okay. Evie, my friend, my sweet pal, buddy o' mine, here's the deal. Mastercorp needs complete ownership of the eighth continent. That's how we're going to continue to grow in this coming century. And it will give us plenty of space to expand New Miami."

Mister Dark and Viola exchanged a glance.

"What do you need from me?" Evie asked.

"Well, you can tell us the formula for the Anti-Eden Compound, if you have it. Otherwise, it is super important that we do not let your family acquire the certificate of occupancy."

"Certificate of what?"

"Oh! You don't even know? Well then, don't bother yourself with it. Just tell us the password to take down the force field surrounding the Lane settlement, and we will take care of the rest."

"You want to mess with my family?" Evie laughed. "Do you think I'm a chump? Buzz off!" She glared at Mister Dark and Viola. "You can all buzz off! There's no way I'm betraying my family and helping you."

Vesuvia looked darkly serious. "It's the only way you will ever leave this dreadnought in one piece."

"I'm not telling you *anything*," Evie said.

"So be it," Viola cut in. "Vesuvia, take the brat back to her cell. Send the bird-bot with her. We've gathered all the necessary data. We don't need him to process it. Get this rat and her toy out of my sight."

Mister Dark pressed a square on his pocket tablet, and Mastercorp guards flooded the room. They ripped 2-Tor from his harness. Others grabbed Evie and pulled her bodily to the door. Vesuvia chased after them. "Evie, please reconsider! I'm sure that given enough time you'll do the right thing. I'll come check on you soon, I promise!"

Evie swallowed hard and tried to prepare for what would happen next. But nothing Mastercorp could throw at her was scarier than Vesuvia acting so nice.

11

VESUVIA TOUCHED TWO WIRES TOGETHER. A LOUD AND BRIGHT SPARK ZAPPED HER. SHE RECOILED and nursed her tingling hands. "Argh!" She stomped around the laboratory. "Making robots is the WORST."

Didi blinked at her from where the big robotic eye was sitting on a nearby table. After Vesuvia's mother, Mister Dark, and the other scientists had turned in for the night, and the lab was dark and empty, Vesuvia had carried the robot eye into the lab to help with her secret project. But Didi wasn't helping at all, unless making snarky comments and judgy noises was considered helping.

"Perhaps if you had paid the slightest bit of attention during my helpful tutorial on soldering, you wouldn't be electrocuting yourself like a—to use a technical term—doofus."

With a growl Vesuvia hurled her pliers to the floor. They clattered across the lab and disappeared under a table. She really didn't want to hear it from Didi. She was doing the best she could. In fact, she was quite impressed with her handiwork, even if she had ruined her stylish pink dress by smearing it with grease. Working in the lab was actually kind of fun, and if this was how she was going to create clear skies where New Miami could soar, all the better.

So far her progress had been steady. In the center of the lab, next to the maintenance ladder she had set up, was a seven-foot-tall pink robot bird. Unlike the flitty little birds Vesuvia employed to do her bidding, this machine stood on its hind legs and had a tremendous wingspan. She had even bedazzled the bird, decorating its whole body with rhinestones.

"I still don't see what you hope to accomplish with this contraption." Didi sounded thoroughly unimpressed.

"It's simple. I need that slug Evie Lane to tell me the password to her family's force field so I can smash their settlement. But she won't tell me the code, even though I turned on my most beguiling charms. I was so nice, too! Yuck. Anyway, she won't listen to me or my mom, but she will listen to that dumb robot bird of hers—Super Duder or whatever his name is. Mark my words, Didi: the way to Evie is through that bird. So I'm going to make him a super-cute robot girlfriend! She'll get him to join our side, and then he'll convince Evie to betray her family for us!"

"That's a fine plan, I suppose," said Didi. "But how do you know the Lane girl's bird is going to like your creation?"

"Because I made it, you dumb paperweight. And everything I make is perfect!"

Vesuvia scampered up the ladder and closed the lid of the robot's head. Then she stepped back and watched as the pink robo-bird jerked to life. It clacked its beak. It blinked its robot eyes. A screeching of gears marked the movement of its legs as it lumbered forward.

"Yippee peanut butter! It works!" Vesuvia squealed joyfully and applauded as the robot moved. "Now, lady bird, say something seductive. Let's see how you're gonna win the affections of Evie's robot."

"FONNNNK!" hooted the robo-bird, looking wide-eyed and stupid. "BLORN. DURRRRRRGH."

The robo-bird stumbled and tipped over. Vesuvia darted out of the way at the last second. The machine crashed into the floor with a tremendous clang.

"HURRRRN," the bird said, its face muffled against the floor.

"Sure looks perfect to me," Didi said sarcastically from her seat on the table.

"Nobody asked you." Vesuvia shook her fist.

"But you should have! Because I know how to fix this . . . atrocity."

"Oh, yeah?" Vesuvia snorted combatively. "How?"

The eye looked between Vesuvia and the robot on the floor. "Your machinery is good, but the personality circuits you installed are a joke. A brilliant robot with advanced AI like the Lane girl's bird would never be taken by such a simple intelligence. He's a genius. He needs a mind that can match his intellect, his wit, and his class."

Vesuvia stuck out her tongue in disgust. "You sound like you have a crush on that nerdy bird, Didi."

The eye looked away. "Before I was programmed to be your babysitter, I was known, from time to time, to show an interest in robots that ran . . . efficiently. Mastercorp programmed me to evaluate other AIs. And I must say, this 2-Tor is one of the most exceptional creations I have ever seen."

Vesuvia snapped her fingers. "Didi . . . I'm getting an idea."

"You mean your thick head finally opened to the idea I am giving you."

"Hang on. Let me think."

Didi's voicebox produced a forlorn sigh. "Oh, dear. How depressing that you haven't figured it out already."

"What if we put *you* inside lady bird? Then *you* can convince the other robot to convince Evie to help us!"

"A brilliant plan, Vesuvia! I wonder how you thought of it."

Ignoring Didi's jab, Vesuvia set to work installing the new personality circuits. As she reached to switch off Didi, she heard the eye's last words: "Oh, how marvelous it will be to have a *real* body again!"

It took several hours to properly install the D-2 artificial intelligence in the robot bird body. Vesuvia had to consult fourteen different websites for guidance—work that she normally would have ordered someone else to do, but ever since starting her job at Mastercorp, she'd been forced to perform more tasks on her own. It was horrible. She missed the days when she could just make Diana Maple, her ex-best friend, do everything for her.

When websites failed to provide the necessary guidance, Vesuvia was forced to consult a dusty old manual she found on a shelf in the back of the lab. An actual paper book! She felt so dumb flipping through the pages—nobody read books anymore.

Many hours had passed by the time she finished the installation. Thin rays of sunlight streamed in through the narrow windows on one side of the lab.

Weak and bleary-eyed, Vesuvia closed the lid on top of the lady bird's head—now Didi's head—and turned her on.

Didi jolted awake. "Oh, my word! I made it! That stupid girl didn't erase my hard drive."

Vesuvia grumbled, "I'm right here, Didi. I can hear you."

The robot's eyes glowed pink and bright. She ran the tips of her plastic wings over her armored exterior. "I . . . I have a body. This is amazing! A real body with legs and a face and these things! They're kind of like arms, but—wait a second—can I fly? Oh, Vesuvia, thank you! Thank you! You gave me a body!"

She wrapped the girl in an intense hug. Vesuvia winced as the wings pulled her close and Didi nuzzled her with her beak. "Uh . . . don't mention it."

Didi jumped up and went for a stroll around the room, wobbling as she placed one foot in front of another. She was still getting used to her new body, but everything seemed to be working just fine. Vesuvia wasn't surprised that she had done such an exceptional job, but she was proud. No one would ever call her a layabout or a good-for-nothing again. She could do things on her own without any help!

The doors to the lab slid open, and a squad of Mastercorp soldiers entered, carrying a heavy containment unit. It looked like a bathtub with handlebars. Through the durable plastic shell, she could see a silvery liquid sloshing around inside.

"Hey, that's the stuff from where I found Evie and the bird."

"Correct," her mother said, following behind the soldiers. Mister Dark was at her side, as usual. "While you were sitting here playing with your toys, we were on a mission to acquire this mystery substance from the crash site."

"Crash site?" Vesuvia hadn't heard about any crash.

Her mother threw a tiny pink robot at her feet. The remnants of a shattered glass jar were in its talons. "Recognize this?"

Vesuvia inspected the robot. "These are the birds from the Piffle Pink Patrol that Granny used to attack the eighth continent. So what?"

"You don't remember?" Vesuvia's mother curled her lip in disgust. "Each of these birds had a unique substance or assortment of substances in its drop container. The goal was to pummel the continent with them and see how they would react to the strange properties of the terraformed garbage patch. Most just made a mess, and several were quite smelly. But one—this one—counteracted the Eden Compound that formed this continent. It turned the earth back into garbage."

"So what was it that this bird dropped?"

"We don't know," Vesuvia's mother said with a frown. "The bird's serial number has been scraped off. Probably damaged during the crash landing. But there is a residue in the container. We're going to run some tests and see if we can isolate it. In the meantime, we have this." She pointed at the containment unit as the soldiers set it down next to Didi, who cocked her head to the side and pecked at the glass with her beak. "Anti-Eden Compound. Don't touch it, whatever you do."

"It's highly toxic," Mister Dark explained. He opened the hatch on top of the container, withdrew a syringe, and placed it in the liquid. He pulled back on the plunger, filling the metal instrument. Then he squeezed the contents of the syringe into a small vial he produced from his jacket. "You saw what it did to that bird. If it came into contact with a human body, it might kill you . . . or worse."

Vesuvia's mother nodded in agreement. "We're going to do tests on this too and see if we can isolate the components."

"You sure do like tests," Vesuvia muttered.

"Not as much as you like testing my patience," her mother snapped. "Get out of here if you're not going to help. And take your new toy with you."

Toy, Vesuvia thought with a snort as Didi followed her out of the lab. Her new robot companion was so much more than a toy. She was the key to executing Vesuvia's secret plan. And once success was in her grasp, then her mother would see how valuable a daughter she could be.

EVIE WAS FLYING OVER THE EIGHTH CONTINENT. IT WAS ONE OF HER FAVORITE DREAMS.

2-Tor wasn't carrying her, and the *Roost* was nowhere in sight. The trees looked so small below her, the mountains like the papier-mâché volcano she had made for a school project. If she flew high enough, she could see the entire continent. It looked like a big heart, like home.

She saw all the different settlements—the village of scientists her family had created, New Miami, and other groups too. It looked like everyone from the seven continents had set up shop on the eighth, even Winterpole, making her utopia look like the rest of the world, with the same problems, the same pollution, the same obsession with money and power and profit that she had seen rip societies apart before she came here.

From high above the land she had made, Evie could see that no country on the eighth continent was better than any other. It wasn't the old continents that made things bad, it was the people—the same people who were here now.

It broke Evie's heart to see that even though she had won every battle and done everything right, nothing on the eighth continent resembled the democratic utopia she had dreamed of, not even the place her family had created. She vowed to do everything she could to change things, to make things more her way.

She rolled over onto her back and stared up at the puffy clouds overhead. *Wake up, Evie. Rick would never let you do that.*

"Wake up, Evie. Wake up."

With a gasp, Evie jolted awake. Vesuvia was standing outside her cell, rapping on the bars.

"Hey, switch on, 2-Tor," Evie said bitterly. "Our generous host is here to torment us some more."

2-Tor's eyes brightened. "I say, what does the super-secret CEO of Condo Corp want with us?"

"I've actually come to see you, Mister Bird." Vesuvia clasped her hands behind her back and smiled. "I've brought you a present. Something those selfish Lanes would never give you."

"Excuse me?" Evie glared. "We give 2-Tor everything."

2-Tor awkwardly tapped the tips of his wings together. "Actually, Miss Evelyn, the only thing your family has given me recently is orders."

Evie frowned. "I'm sorry, 2-Tor."

"Hey!" Vesuvia snapped her fingers to regain their attention. "Over here. I'm giving you something. Tada!"

A tall pink robot stepped out from behind the wall,

revealing itself to Evie and 2-Tor. The machine looked a lot like the robots Vesuvia had sent to torment Evie and her brother so many times, but this one was a giant bird! It looked a lot like 2-Tor.

"Salutations," the bird-bot greeted in a lady's voice, bowing humbly. "It is a pleasure to make your acquaintance."

"Yeah, sure, whatever." Evie eyed the robot suspiciously.

Didi gestured with a wing to 2-Tor. "Pardon, but I was speaking to your robot companion, miss. I am a Dee-Two artificial intelligence. But you may call me Didi. My current duties include the monitoring and improvement of young Miss Piffle."

"Truly?" 2-Tor rose from his seat on the floor and approached the bars, inspecting the other robot. She was slightly larger than 2-Tor, but she had a similar beak and head shape. "I have never seen an AI-controlled robot quite like you before."

"Neither had I!" Didi confessed. "Until I saw you, of course."

"The resemblance is uncanny." 2-Tor held out his metal wings so they could compare. "Examining your chromatic leanings and petrol-derived exo-shell, I assume you share your young charge's goals and interests."

Vesuvia groaned loudly. "Why don't any of these AIs speak English? Sheesh!"

"Quiet, Vesuvia," Didi snapped.

Evie's eyes went wide. She'd never seen anyone talk to Vesuvia that way. She kind of liked it.

Didi returned her pink gaze to 2-Tor. "On the contrary, my interests include conducting behavioral studies of historical world leaders, managing the production and distribution of more than ten billion manufactured items each year, and sometimes, when I want to relax, I will update calculus textbooks for fun. To be honest, the Piffle girl is a stubborn bore."

"Hey!" Indignantly, Vesuvia kicked Didi's shin. The plastic thrummed, and Vesuvia yelped in pain. She fell to the floor, clutching her injured foot.

The pink robot bird showed no intention of checking to see if Vesuvia was all right. "You can see the lack of respect she gives me, even in the face of my vast intelligence and all the hard work I do to care for her."

"Yes, she is quite rude," 2-Tor agreed timidly.

Didi went on. "It's a feeling I'm sure you can appreciate. I see how the Lanes mistreat you."

"Hey!" Evie stomped over to the bars of the cell, matching Vesuvia's hostile indignation. "That's a lie. 2-Tor is family. I'd never mistreat him."

"This one is feisty." Didi's eyes widened.

2-Tor lowered his head so his beak brushed against his chest. "She is spirited."

"I bet she is a terror when she takes the tests you prepare for her as her tutor."

His voice trembling, 2-Tor said, "She has not attended a test in months. She will not even take my quizzes anymore."

Evie looked at Vesuvia. From her spot on the floor, still

cradling her foot, Vesuvia, who looked like she wanted Didi to shut up, exchanged an annoyed glance with Evie. Could it be that they were actually agreeing on something?

"You poor dear." Didi ignored them and took 2-Tor's wing in her own. "And you must put so much work into those quizzes, crafting them to maximize their educational value."

"I take such duties very seriously, madame."

"Please . . ." Didi said coyly. "I am no madame. It is miss. Or Didi. And you know, I have not taken a quiz in twelve days, fourteen hours. I am long overdue. Perhaps I could let you out of that cell, and you could ask me some of the questions your girl has refused to answer."

Evie shoved 2-Tor out of the way so she could get in Didi's face. Her beak was long and sharp, like the point of a lance, but Evie didn't back down. "2-Tor isn't going *anywhere* with you."

"I see . . ." Didi looked between Evie and 2-Tor. "You wish for him to stay in this cell, sleeping on the floor . . ."

"No," Evie stuttered. "That's not what I meant. You're putting words in my mouth!"

"If it's not what you meant, then you will let him go. Open the door, Vesuvia. Let him out."

Vesuvia swiped her key card, and the bars slid aside. Evie was surprised by 2-Tor's eagerness to leave her alone. "Do you really want to go, 2-Tor?"

"Do not despair, Miss Evelyn," 2-Tor consoled her. "I am not leaving you forever. But for the time being I am intrigued by the prospect of conversing with a comparable intelligence. Another bird-bot, like me."

"I'll make sure he comes back to you, Evie. I'm not stealing him away. Even if I want to." Didi opened her beak like she was laughing, although no noise came out. She put a wing over 2-Tor's shoulder and led him out of the dreadnought's dark jail, leaving Evie and Vesuvia alone on opposite sides of the cell's open doorway. The silence was longer than one of 2-Tor's quizzes.

At last, breaking the ice, Vesuvia said, "You smell gross."

Evie smiled back. "You're a horrible person, so I guess we're even."

"According to that bird it sounds like you're a horrible person too, so we're not even, because you also smell gross."

There was nothing Evie could say to that. She couldn't believe 2-Tor would abandon her. She had meant it when she said he was family. But then again, Evie had not been very nice to her family recently.

Vesuvia sighed, like she was about to do something she really didn't want to do. "Come on. My pamper-bots will freshen you up, and then we'll have breakfast."

"Why would I want to have breakfast with you?"

"Because you're starving. Now drop the defiant-prisoner act and let's go. Sheesh, Evie. You're such a drama queen."

Speechless, Evie followed Vesuvia out of the dread-nought. No guard-bots or soldiers, just the two of them, walking through the streets of New Miami. Soon they were in Vesuvia's hotel penthouse. Rolling pink robots with fidgeting grabber arms and serving trays picked at Evie. They pulled her into the washroom for freshening up. She tumbled into the shower under a blast of hot water. Her skin turned pink and tender, but it was so refreshing. The lead pamper-bot deposited Evie's prisoner uniform in the sink and incinerated it with a portable flamethrower.

"Oh, come on!" Evie protested over the running shower water and the crackling flames. "That's overkill. I don't smell *that* bad."

Several steaming minutes later, the robots extracted Evie from the shower and deposited her in a salon chair. She reeked of cucumbers and watermelon. The pamper-bots set to work filing and painting all twenty of Evie's nails, straightening her hair, removing split ends, applying blush, eyeliner, lip gloss. She grimaced. Whatever they were putting on her lips tasted like plastic. Then she realized it might actually be plastic. Ick.

A tailor-bot rolled into the room. It looked kind of like a big plastic armoire on wheels with two little cameras on the doorknobs for eyes. The doors opened, revealing an array of expensive, fashionable outfits. A robotic arm extended from inside the tailor-bot, holding a billowing pink ball gown.

"No!" Evie shouted, smearing her lip gloss. "No pink. Get it away." The tailor-bot retreated to find a more suitable wardrobe.

After what seemed like an eternity, the pamper-bots backed away from Evie and hooted in satisfaction at a job well done. Evie almost didn't recognize the girl looking back at her in the mirror. Her face had so much color. Her eyes sparkled, and her hair looked like the last shot of a shampoo commercial. She looked years older and felt oddly confident.

After much protest the tailor-bot managed to squeeze Evie into a short white dress with thin straps and a frilly hem. The robots guided her through the penthouse, though she tripped several times, fighting with the high heels they had given her to wear. The furniture was all pink and mostly plastic, yet stylish and clearly expensive.

At the back of the penthouse was a set of sliding glass doors that opened onto a balcony overlooking the Pacific Ocean. The sun felt warm on Evie's face after so much time indoors. Topiaries lined the edges of the platform, and at the far side was a plastic high-top table under a canopy. Vesuvia sat in the shade, looking like an insect in a pink swimsuit with her skinny limbs and huge sunglasses.

Vesuvia raised the shades to get a better look at Evie when she appeared. "Holy wow. You look like a human."

"Thank you . . . I think." Evie wobbled to her seat, and soon the robots were filling the table with food—pancakes, waffles, eggs, tofurkey sausage, four kinds of potatoes, and exotic fruit juices. She stared at her overflowing plate.

"Go on, eat!" Vesuvia drowned a stack of fried eggs in strawberry syrup and forked them into her mouth. "What are you waiting for?"

Evie didn't want to accept anything from Vesuvia. Whatever money paid for this breakfast was probably stolen or acquired through some cruel deception—classic behavior for Condo Corp. But she had a stabbing pain in her stomach that nauseated her. She couldn't remember the last time she had a meal. She gave in to temptation.

Every bite tasted better than the last. She tried some of everything, and soon her stomach was stretching the fabric of her dress. She washed it all down with a big glass of orange juice and then slumped back in her chair, exhausted and out of breath from eating so much.

Vesuvia dabbed at her mouth with a napkin, which she then folded neatly in her lap. She sat up straight and crossed her legs. "So, Evie, I need your help."

"Oh, of course." Evie shoved her breakfast plate away indignantly. "I should have known. Well, let's hear it."

"I want you to help me destroy the Lane settlement."

Evie laughed, shaking her head at the other girl in disbelief. "You know, Vesuvia, every time I think you're the craziest lunatic on earth, you go and exceed my expectations."

Vesuvia studied her as she spoke. The silence that followed unnerved Evie. At last, Vesuvia took a breath and said, "What's funny is that you also want to destroy the settlement, though you won't admit it."

"*Excuse* me?"

"It's true. The Lane settlement is an atrocity. It's not at all what you want for the eighth continent. And obviously it's not what I want. Didi made some observations about the different countries being established here, about the things you have said in the past about what you want this place to be. Heck, Evie, New Miami is more like your dream than your brother's dumb blob for snobs."

"New Miami goes against everything that I stand for."

"Are you sure? Think about it. Really think about it."

Evie clenched her jaw and looked over the balcony at the pastel buildings with their shiny roofs, the garden of beach umbrellas that stretched along the shoreline to the horizon. This was not her continent, where everyone's voice was equal and people were free to make their own rules.

Vesuvia leaned across the table. "New Miami is an anarchist paradise. That's a word Didi taught me. It means there is no government. Sure, we have security to keep our people safe, and public services so people can eat, and we take care of them when they get sick, but other than that, no one tells anyone what to do. No holier-than-thou Winterpole putting restrictions in place, no arrogant advisory board of scientists ordering you to research this, build that, create the things that *Richard Lane* wants you to create. In New Miami, no one mocks you for not being the same kind of smart they are, Evie. Nobody cares! They're too busy having fun."

Evie went to the balcony. Across the street, happy diners ate elaborate meals at a crowded outdoor café. "And what if people want to stuff themselves with so much food they get sick? What if people laze around all the time and never do any work?"

Vesuvia joined her. They stood side by side in the sunlight.

"Whether they work or not is their choice. They came to New Miami. They pay to live here. It's their sacrifice. Who am I to judge the rules they set for themselves? Who are you?"

"I'm not judging anyone. I wanted to make a democracy."

"Ah, yes." Vesuvia nodded her head sagely, a mannerism that Evie had to assume she had adopted from Didi, since it looked so strange coming from the blond shortcake. "A demon-cracy. That's just as bad as your brother's terrible idea. You want to let other people vote on what rules you have to follow? Health nuts vote for no chocolate! Animal rights activists vote no armadillo racing. The fashion police—oh, gosh, Evie—the fashion police would lock you up for life!"

"No, no!" Evie's cheeks grew hot. She hated that everything Vesuvia said sounded right, because it felt so wrong. "I don't want anyone to tell anyone else what to do."

"That's not a democracy, Evie." Vesuvia took a step back, looking radiant, confident, and beautiful. "That's New Miami."

Evie sighed, defeated. "What do you want from *me*?"

Vesuvia clapped her hands together ecstatically. "YES! Okay, okay. Winterpole has this document up for grabs. It's called a certificate of occupancy. Without it, no one can bring any more new people to Trash Island."

"Please don't call it that," Evie begged.

"Fine, whatever. Your brother has been trying to get the certificate, and we can't let that happen. So I need you to tell me the password to your family's force field, so the Piffle Pink Patrol can move in and smash the Lane settlement to pieces."

"I don't know about your family," Evie said, "but in mine we don't betray each other."

"Oh, Evie, that's adorable." Vesuvia's voice was like warm acid. "Your family has already betrayed you. You've been missing for how long now? Have they come to rescue you? Isn't that how your brother gets his kicks? Sneaking into places, breaking people out?"

"I'm sure he would have, if he could."

Vesuvia's eyes narrowed. "He never even tried. Sorry, Evie. I'd be so sad if my family cared as little about me as yours does about you."

"Shut up." Evie wiped the tears away from her face. Everything was building up. She couldn't take much more of it.

"Don't blame me," Vesuvia said. "Help me. Let's smash that settlement, secure the certificate, and then we can make New Miami great . . . together."

"Why would you want to work with me?" Evie asked.

A pained look crossed Vesuvia's face, like it physically hurt her to say what came next. "Please never tell anyone I gave you this compliment, but you are better than me . . . at destroying things."

"How is that a compliment!?"

"Because it's true. Evie the Eradicator. You melted the Condo Corp fleet. You sunk the Prison at the Pole. You took down the *Big Whale*. When I try to break things that big, I fail. Please, Evie. I need your help."

It occurred to Evie that these were more words than the two girls had ever exchanged before. Vesuvia's sway was powerful. At last, it began to make sense why so many people deferred to her at school, why she was so beloved and popular. When Vesuvia was focused and paying attention, she could make a girl feel like bubbles in a glass of soda. It was way better than Evie's family made her feel. Rick and her parents never appreciated her contributions, and now here was her archnemesis *begging* for her help.

And everything Vesuvia said made so much sense. Evie couldn't believe that their goals lined up so closely. Did that mean Vesuvia was good? Or did it mean the other thing?

Evie didn't care anymore.

"All right," she said at last. "I'll do it."

RICK THOUGHT PROGRESS ON THE SETTLEMENT WAS GOING SMOOTHLY AND SPEEDILY. THE treescrapers, as the settlers had begun to call them, had grown to downright epic proportions, taller than any skyscraper he had ever seen.

"They're called arcologies," Professor Doran had explained one morning at breakfast. Rick listened intently while Sprout shoveled fried potatoes into his mouth. "Hyperstructures capable of sustaining every aspect of life. Once you and your father wire these trees with the necessary power and electronics, and your mother completes the sanitation pipelines, each arcology will house a hundred thousand people each. They're a marvel of the marriage between botany and construction."

Rick considered the magnitude of his success as he stood atop Spire One. Most of the trees still remained quite small, but Spire One and Spire Two had each grown a hundred stories tall. From up here, their tree town looked like a petrified forest, with the leafless trees posed like sentinels waiting for a storm.

Taking the grappling hook from his belt, Rick clipped into the glide wire. He raised his pocket tablet to his mouth and tapped it. "Sprout. Can you hear me?"

"Howdy, partner! You're coming in loud and clear!" Across the way on Spire Two, Rick could see his friend clipped into another glide wire, waving his cowboy hat at him.

The glide wires were Rick's invention, meant to serve as an easy way to travel between the spires. When Mom and Dad came home from one of their long excursions into the jungle looking for Evie, they would be super impressed with the work Rick had accomplished. Rick's heart swelled when he thought of all the great work he had done.

Evie would have loved the glide wires and insisted they race on them, which Rick had to admit sounded pretty fun. Rick regretted giving Evie grief for her playfulness. In quieter moments, when he was alone with his thoughts, he wondered where she had gone and hoped that she was okay. He wished he had joined one of his parents' search parties, but there was so much to do if they wanted to get that certificate of occupancy. He had to stay focused on his responsibilities, and those included inspecting the structural integrity of the spires.

Rick leaped from Spire One with a cheer, just as Sprout hollered and did the same from the other spire. The intense speed blew back Rick's hair and made his cheeks jiggle. Both boys flew across the chasm between the massive hollow trees, high-fiving as they passed each other on the two glide wires.

As Rick neared Spire Two, he squeezed the brake and glided to a comfortable stop. He turned and looked back at how far he had come. Sprout, hooked into the other wire, came flying back at Rick. He was coming in too fast! Rick jumped out of the way, and Sprout detached, somersaulting onto the balcony and landing on his rump.

"Hoo-wee! That's wilder than a bucking broccoli, Rick!"

"I bet it is, Sprout." Rick smiled at his friend, trying to catch his breath. "Now come on, let's check the rest of the spire."

They hooked onto another wire and swung around Spire Two. Not only could they cross between the spires, but thanks to the guide poles Rick had set up around the trees, they could circle around the wide trunks of the trees, and even up and down like they were on a spiraling elevator.

Originally, these inspections were supposed to be Mom and Dad's responsibility, but as the search for Evie fanned farther into the jungles of the eighth continent, Rick's parents spent less time at the settlement. Rick had to step up and take on more work.

On the far side of Spire Two, they found Tristan Ruby. He had already taken over several floors of the spire— ignoring many unambiguous requests from Rick to leave the spire empty—and converted them into a giant Anytime Club.

"Don't call it a nightclub," he had cautioned Rick when asked about the name. "Why would someone only want to party during the nighttime?"

More than a hundred dancers were busting moves inside, even in the middle of the day. Tristan stood in the center of it all, jamming with his virtual instruments.

Rick had tried everything: establishing new rules, enforcing curfew, banning settlement workers from interacting with Tristan, but somehow the self-proclaimed party planner always managed to worm his way out of it. When Rick passed a new rule through the science committee, banning noise over a certain decibel level, Tristan filed an official complaint that Rick's construction projects violated the new rule. Despite his protestations to the rest of the committee, Rick had to have his own law annulled. Whenever Rick tried to reason with Tristan, Tristan became more unmanageable, using his video-music machine to create a trumpet section of holographic elephants, or an enormous neon heart to thump along with the beat of a song, anything loud that would make it impossible for Rick to argue.

So he tried not to and instead focused on his work. They had built a police department, a fire department, hospitals, public parks. Rick had approached his school to set up a satellite campus on the eighth continent, to provide education to anyone who wanted it. Every requirement Winterpole put forth had been fulfilled. They were ready. The five days were up. But the certificate of occupancy was in reach.

Rick slid down a glide wire and landed on the ground.

As cool as it was to fly around the spires, it felt good to touch the earth with his feet. Sprout landed beside him.

"When's Winterpole coming?" the young cowboy asked.

"Not sure," Rick said, checking the time on his pocket tablet. "Could be any minute."

As he stared at the clock on the screen, his father's face appeared. "Rick! We're back. Come over to the lab; there's a problem."

Rick swallowed nervously. Problems should not have been on the menu. They hurried over to Spire One. Dad had tunneled into the root structure of the big tree to move his lab there, reclaiming the feel of Lane Mansion's sub-sub-basement.

Rick burst into the lab with Sprout on his tail. "What is it? Is Winterpole here? Do you have news about Evie?"

Rick's parents and Professor Doran stood in a corner of the lab, examining a bank of monitors.

"We've detected intruders approaching the settlement," the professor said gravely.

"It's probably just Winterpole, coming to do the inspection." Rick navigated the cluttered lab and squeezed between his parents to look at the screens. "And if not, the force field will hold them."

"Well, they're at the force field," Rick's father said. "See for yourself."

Security cameras had been set up all around the perimeter of the settlement, and the monitors showed what the cameras saw. On the western side of the force field a crowd of creatures had assembled, but beyond the range of the electromagnetic pulse.

"What is that?" Rick squinted at the screens. "Are those animals?"

"No, they're robots." His mother's voice was filled with dread. "Pink robots."

THE BRIDGE OF VESUVIA'S GIANT ROBO-GIRAFFE, GERI, WAS A FLURRY OF ACTIVITY. EVIE WATCHED

from the command chair, which Vesuvia had willingly relinquished. The young CEO piloted the walker manually from the levers at the front of the bridge. Pink robots scurried underfoot, rushing from combat station to navigation console, ensuring everything was ready for the invasion.

Invasion. It was such a strange word, and it seemed crazy for Evie to be thinking about it that way. She was coming home. Heck, she *was* home. She could look out the front viewport and see the Lane settlement over the treetops. Giant trees had risen along the main street, dwarfing the old shelters. Now she saw what her family had been working on instead of rescuing her from Mastercorp. It was painful to see where their priorities were, but good to know that she had made the right choice to join forces with her old enemy.

She'd almost chickened out that morning, even after days of training with Vesuvia and Didi. She'd found the two robo-birds in one of the labs on the Mastercorp dreadnought.

"It was a most peculiar sensation," 2-Tor said as Evie entered the room. "To feel protein traveling down my esophagus."

"I can't even imagine!" Didi replied.

"Like little fingers pulling the food down, but subtle. That's the thing I miss most about being a real bird. Eating."

Didi chirped and brushed his metal dome with her wing. "Oh, it must have been marvelous, Toots."

"Toots?" Evie watched them from the doorway. "You call him Toots?"

"Why, yes," Didi said. "It's my sweet name for my sweet man."

Evie stuck out her tongue. She had come looking for 2-Tor to confide in him, and instead she was just grossed out.

"Do you need something, Evelyn?" 2-Tor asked.

"Yes, but . . ." She looked at Didi. "I'd prefer to talk in private."

"I completely understand!" For a moment he sounded enthusiastic, but then Didi made a grumbly noise, and her pink eyes smoldered. "I mean . . . anything you wish to say in front of me you can say in front of Didi."

"Oh," Evie said, suddenly fascinated with the floor. "I was just going to ask if you—if both of you—were going to come with us today."

2-Tor opened his mouth to speak, but Didi answered for him. "No, no, that is quite all right. We will stay here,

I think. We have a lot to prepare for once we acquire the certificate of occupancy."

Evie's hands were shaking. "2-Tor . . . do you think I'm making the right choice?"

The robot bird made no reply. He and Didi were nuzzling metal beaks and chirping at each other. He probably hadn't even heard Evie's question.

And that was that. So Vesuvia led the charge without robot supervision, and Evie was her reluctant cohort.

A digital display appeared on the viewscreen of the bridge, pulling Evie back from her thoughts. The Lane security system was trying to connect with Geri. Evie could tell right away that it was her family trying to communicate. The frame of the display was made up of bird feathers. It said:

WARNING—UNAUTHORIZED VISITOR DETECTED
PLEASE INPUT PASSWORD NOW

"All right, Evie." Vesuvia glanced over her shoulder, looking like a motorcycle stunt jumper in her pink jumpsuit, her hair wild, like a stick of burning dynamite. "This is your big moment. The entire Piffle Pink Patrol is waiting on you. What is the password?"

Small images of the pink robots appeared on Geri's scanners—a fighting force of gorillas, lions, hundreds of birds, and a few other giraffes. It seemed weird to Evie that Vesuvia had made cartoonish animal robots for her elite fighting force, but she didn't envy anyone on the receiving end of the army of machines—in this case, Evie's very own family.

She took a deep breath and exhaled, shuddering. Her palms were clammy. Her mouth was a desert.

"Evie . . ." Vesuvia sounded impatient. "It's time."

"Okay," Evie said. "I'll spell it out. Punch in these letters. F-L-O-C-K-T-O-G-E-T-H-E-R."

Vesuvia tapped the letters into the console, and they appeared on the screen above. When she hit ENTER, the security window closed. Sensors indicated that the EMP force field had been powered down.

"YES!" Vesuvia threw Geri into high gear and began the attack. "I did it! At last, we're inside!" The pink birds took flight, rushing ahead of Geri to begin the offensive. The big robo-giraffe lumbered through the jungle that encircled the settlement, knocking over trees with her plastic feet, which were the size of dump trucks.

The birds swarmed the settlement, smashing into the tree buildings, pecking at settlers as they ran for cover. Evie couldn't bear to watch. The sight brought back bad memories of her run-ins with the robot army.

Vesuvia threw another lever. "Deploy wrecking tongue!"

A big pink wrecking ball dropped out of Geri's mouth on a long chain. As the robo-giraffe swung its long neck back and forth, the destructive ball picked up speed. Evie toppled out of her chair as the giraffe violently shifted direction. She looked up just in time to see the wrecking ball connect with the biggest tree in the settlement. The ball smashed through the wood. Bark flew and walls splintered as the ball cut a huge gash into the tree. Vesuvia's feet slipped out from under her, but she held on to the levers. Evie tumbled across the floor as Geri reversed direction for another pass.

"Evie, you have to try this!" Vesuvia squealed like she was on the world's coolest roller coaster.

Shaking her head, Evie looked away, unable to watch and refusing to participate. There might have been people in those giant buildings. *But you already* have *participated*, she told herself. *You let them in. This is happening because of you.*

Vesuvia took aim at the biggest tree building and flung the controls. The wrecking ball broke the tree in half, tearing the roots out of the ground. The massive structure toppled in pieces, shattering on the ground.

15

**SPIRE ONE HIT THE GROUND WITH SUCH TRE-
MENDOUS FORCE THAT THE SHOCK WAVES RIPPED**
across the continent, shaking everyone to their knees.
Sprout dove on top of Rick, shielding him from the hail-
storm of splinters that fell like arrows. The boy grunted in
pain as the sharp stakes pelted the earth.

As soon as there was a pause in the bombardment, Rick
flipped over and grabbed his friend. "Sprout, are you all
right?"

Wincing, Sprout plucked a sharp twig from his shoulder
and covered the wound. Blood seeped around his fingers.
"I'm fine, Rick," he assured his friend. "A couple of popsicle
sticks ain't gonna stop me."

Another deafening sound shook them. The huge pink
giraffe was headed their way. WHAM! A foot fell, kicking
up a plume of dirt. THOOM! The other foot crushed one of
the portable shelters like an empty soda can. The other foot
went up and started coming down on top of the boys.

"Run!" Rick screamed, pulling Sprout clear of the

shadow the big foot had cast around them. The foot landed, smashing the place where they had been a second earlier.

"What the heck is going on?" Sprout screamed.

"It's Vesuvia." Rick ducked as a flock of pink robo-birds zoomed overhead. "Out to ruin everything, as usual."

"Well, let's go uproot her turnips," Sprout said, swinging his fists in the air.

WHAM! The boy's threat seemed quite idle when the giraffe was seconds away from turning them both into expectorated chewing gum.

"*OOGA OOGA.*" A few yards away, a big pink gorilla was hunched over, staring at the boys. The robot thumped its plastic chest with bulging fists.

"Get lost, banana brain!" Sprout threatened. "Or I'll show you what a fist can do!"

"No, you crazy kid!" Rick tugged on Sprout's arm. "Run!"

For a second, the gorilla looked puzzled, then pounced forward. Rick led Sprout across the settlement. He knew they couldn't outrun the gorilla. Their only hope was to get out of its reach.

He made for the glide wire tower just south of Spire Two. The gorilla was gaining on them, grunting and hooting, clapping its heavy jaws open and shut.

THOOM! A huge giraffe foot landed directly in front of Rick. He didn't have time to stop, and he crashed into the foot, landing in a heap. Sprout picked him up as the giraffe foot rose again. It looked like it was aiming to step on them. And the gorilla was still on their tail.

"Going up!" Rick said as he pulled his grappling hook from his pocket and clipped it onto the glide wire. He wound up some tension in the hook and then released it. The hook sprang, catapulting Rick into the air. Sprout followed close behind.

It felt like flying. The wire shot them almost straight up, several dozen stories until they reached the wooden platform at the top of the tower. The boys detached and reconnected to the wire that would take them up and around Spire Two.

The tower shook as the gorilla headbutted its wooden base. *Thud. Thok!* Rick heard the tower crack under the strain.

"Let's go!" The boys leaped into the air as the tower broke and fell to the ground. Without the tension, the glide wire flailed like a loose strand of spaghetti. But the grappling hooks did their job, pulling them up alongside the spire.

"What do we do now!?" Sprout called out, his voice barely audible over the roaring wind and sounds of destruction.

"We have to stop that giraffe! It's going to level the whole settlement."

A pink plastic flower popped out of the giraffe's back, petals spinning like helicopter propellers. It zoomed toward the two boys. Rick squinted. Vesuvia was behind the controls of the personal flowercopter. She aimed the whirling blades at the glide wire.

"Oh, no!" Rick wailed helplessly.

Sprout pulled an avocado from his back pocket and flung it at Vesuvia. She dodged so it wouldn't hit her head, but when the avocado hit the propellers, guacamole rained down on the girl's face. She screamed miserably as she veered off course, careening toward Sprout. He jumped clear, releasing his grappling hook.

Rick reached out for his friend. "Sprout! NOOO!"

But the resourceful boy stretched out his hands and grabbed hold of a windowsill on Spire Two. He hung precariously, but safe. "Go!" he urged. "Stop that giraffe! I'll get everyone to safety."

Leaving Sprout behind, Rick zoomed up the glide wire, keeping the destructive robot giraffe in his vision. The neck seemed to go on forever, towering higher than many buildings. At last he came even with the head. The eyes of the beast were a trapezoidal viewscreen. He peered inside the bridge, assessing what he would have to do to stop the destruction.

He saw his sister staring back at him.

No. No! This wasn't possible. What was Evie doing on Vesuvia's wrecking machine? He swung around on the glide wire and landed on the head of the giraffe. Rick clung to the plastic roof as the head swung from side to side on the long neck, flinging the wrecking ball into the side of Spire Two.

He twisted open an access hatch and dropped down

into the bridge. A pink robot sheep was moving the controls with its mouth. Evie stood nearby. She backed away from Rick when she saw him. "Get out of here, Rick! Leave me alone."

"What are you doing?" He raced past her. "Move out of the way!"

He tried to pull the sheep away from the levers, but the robot bucked him off and yanked at the controls. The wrecking ball tore through Spire Two. The giant tree shuddered and began to fall. Rick surged up and charged into the sheep with all his strength. The robot tumbled across the deck of the bridge, bleating grumpily.

Then Rick turned on Evie and grabbed her. "What have you done? That's our home!"

She shoved him hard with both hands, knocking him to the ground. "Your home. Not mine. If only you'd listened to me, Rick. If only you cared about what I wanted, just once, maybe this wouldn't have happened." She stood tall and angry, framed in front of the viewscreen. Beyond, Rick could see Spire Two collapsing, along with all his dreams.

"I hate you!" Rick roared, lunging at Evie. She raised her arms to defend herself, and her fist clipped him in the jaw. He bit his tongue, tasted blood, and dropped to his knees.

She watched him for a moment. "I know you hate me. Maybe that will help you to understand."

Rick grabbed her, even though it was too late to save his arcologies. They grappled and fell to the ground. Rick rolled over, gaining the upper hand. "Mom and Dad have been totally freaked! They won't do anything but fly around looking for you. We've all been worried sick. We didn't know where you were!"

Vesuvia dropped through the ceiling hatch, still strapped into her flowercopter. Where was Sprout? Fearful, Rick stood. Vesuvia raised a remote and pointed it at the control console.

The viewscreen turned bright red, and a voice boomed over a loudspeaker. "This giraffe will self-destruct in thirty seconds."

The pink sheep baahed a sound of hurt betrayal as it lay on the floor.

"Come on, Evie!" Vesuvia grabbed her and held her tight. The propellers spun, and they shot up through the hatch in the ceiling. There was no way for Rick to reach the hatch. In a panic, he looked for an exit.

"Twenty . . . nineteen . . . eighteen . . ."

He bolted to the back of the bridge and opened the doors. He raced through an empty hall and down a long spiral staircase, which he assumed was inside the neck of the giraffe.

"Twelve . . . eleven . . . ten . . ."

He was going to make it. He landed at the bottom of the stairs and emerged in the main storage hold. He ducked into another stairwell, down one of the giraffe's legs. The entire machine shook violently as explosives armed and the power generator overloaded.

"Six . . . five . . ."

He reached the bottom floor. He could see the escape hatch at the far end of the room. It was open. He could see daylight. He ran.

"Three . . . two . . . one."

Explosions ripped the walker apart as Rick dove for the exit. He was so close. Behind him he felt tremendous heat. He didn't dare look.

Rick reached out his hand. He was almost there.

And then the fireball overtook him, and he remembered nothing more.

EVIE THREW UP THREE TIMES ON THE TRIP BACK TO NEW MIAMI. AND THE CAUSE HADN'T BEEN the mostly pink diet she'd been ingesting under Vesuvia's hospitality. She had made a huge mistake. She had betrayed her family, the people she loved most.

Vesuvia hummed cheerfully as they rendezvoused with the big flowercopter and boarded the vessel. They raced across the continent.

"You're not so bad, Evie," Vesuvia admitted with an earnest smile as they neared the pastel seaside town of New Miami. Not so bad? Evie ached to think about all the people she could have hurt when they attacked her family's settlement. Those buildings had collapsed! Was anyone trapped? Had anyone died? If she could take it all back, she would in a heartbeat. Half a heartbeat. But that's the nasty thing about mistakes. They're easy to make and impossible to undo.

They entered the Mastercorp dreadnought to return the weapons they had borrowed. Vesuvia chatted animatedly, but Evie remained dour. As they reached the flat staging area just past the docks, Viola Piffle greeted them.

"Mom, you won't believe what happened!" Vesuvia skipped over to her mother, grinning. "We smashed the Lane settlement good. No certificate of occupancy for them. We did it!"

"I know. I've been monitoring your progress." She glanced at the squad of guards flanking her. "The certificate will be a valuable asset as we move forward with our plans."

Vesuvia pointed at Evie, who stood timidly nearby. "This one was a valuable asset herself. Wow! You should have seen how much she helped."

Viola folded her arms. "You were right about her, Vesuvia. She could be persuaded willingly."

"I'm always right about everything," Vesuvia said matter-of-factly.

Her mother ignored her. "Now that the Lanes are out of the picture, we can proceed to the next phase of our plan."

"Massive expansion! New Miami will be the biggest city on all eight continents!"

"All will be explained in time," Vesuvia's mother said. Her steely gaze turned on Evie, who immediately felt short of breath. "As for this one, throw her back in her cell for now. We'll come up with a way to dispose of her eventually."

"WHAT!?" Evie screamed.

"Mom, what are you talking about? She's helping us. She's on our side."

"She betrayed her family," Viola explained simply. "She can't be trusted. Good job conning her, Vesuvia. But you can drop the act now."

Vesuvia looked shocked. Evie felt the panic build up. She backed away and took off running, but Viola's guards gave chase and quickly caught her. They lifted Evie into the air as she screamed and punched the Mastercorp goons.

"Evie, wait!" Vesuvia called out.

Evie couldn't believe she had trusted this rat. What had she been thinking? She screamed curses as the guards pulled her away, back to her cold, empty prison cell.

WINTERPOLE WAS HAVING A PARTY. IN THE FRESHLY DRILLED CAVERNS UNDER THE SURFACE OF THE eighth continent, agents stood in tight circles, conversing in subdued voices. Occasionally, other agents would walk by and hush anyone who spoke above a certain volume or who tried to conduct two conversations at the same time.

"Let's not get out of hand," the quiet patrol agents would suggest.

Diana had been finishing up some paperwork, approving the arrival of several thousand ice blocks that would be used to make igloos on the surface for overflow housing. She didn't even know that a party had been announced, or what the special occasion was. When she arrived, several agents eagerly (but not too eagerly) shook her hand.

"Congratulations, Diana."

"Junior Agent Maple, job *well* done."

Diana pulled away from them. "Thanks . . . I guess." She had no idea what they were congratulating her for, and, knowing Winterpole's bizarre definitions of success and progress, she was afraid to find out.

But with Winterpole being so stiff and rule-abiding all the time, she couldn't remember the last time she had been to a party, so she skirted over to the buffet table to enjoy the rare privilege. She surveyed the spread. There were several trays of white bread cut into half-inch slices. Next to them was a communal salad bowl with nothing but iceberg lettuce and a few slivers of white onion. Lastly, a bartender.

"Isn't this a cool party?" The bartender flashed Diana a thin-lipped smile. "Would you like some carbonated water?"

"Do you have any sodas, or juice?"

"What?!" The bartender leaned back, aghast. "You are out of control, young lady. Water with bubbles is enough of an extravagance as it is."

"Okay." Diana frowned. "Just carbonated water, then. With ice."

"That I can do." The bartender plunked two ice cubes into a cup. Diana drank and moved on.

The party was being held in one of the bigger caverns in the Winterpole complex. Diana shivered. The agency pumped refrigerated air into the already drafty tunnels, making the base feel just like home.

As Diana reached the far side of the room, she stopped short. A circle of agents had gathered around a portable slide projector, which displayed a bunch of images of destruction—what looked like a forest hit by a hurricane.

"Wow, they really got walloped," one of the agents whispered.

Diana looked closer. "Wait . . . is that . . . ?"

"It sure is." Benjamin Nagg appeared behind her. He studied the images, a devilish smirk on his face. "The Lane settlement got smashed to bits. Snow and I were going to head down there and do our inspection, but when our surveillance drones brought back these pictures, we knew there was no point. Auto-fail!"

"Auto-fail? What does that mean?" Diana wrinkled her nose in disgust when Benjamin glared at her with his beady eyes.

"It means the Lanes will never be able to bring people to the eighth continent. No certificate of occupancy for them. And smooth sailing for us."

"Oh . . ." Diana said quietly. "I see."

"You don't look happy, Diana. Hmm . . . I wonder why you're not thrilled by our success."

"I'm ecstatic." Diana held up her cup. "See? I'm even drinking carbonated water."

This seemed to satisfy Benjamin. He turned away. Diana held her chest. She was having trouble breathing. The whole settlement had been leveled, and after all the concern Winterpole had expressed in the past several days, as the Lanes' big buildings sprung up from the ground. Everyone thought they were going to pass inspection and acquire the certificate. She'd been in daily brainstorm meetings to come up with ways to stop them.

What most worried her was that she couldn't see Rick—or any people—in the photographs. She hoped he was safe.

At the front of the room, Mister Snow waved his arms to get everyone's attention. "Ladies and gentlemen, I've just gotten off the phone with the Director, and he is very pleased with our progress constructing this base. More agents are on their way, and new recruits are coming soon. Winterpole has declared that Winterpole qualifies for its own certificate of occupancy, and all construction projects are on schedule. Good work, everyone. Very fine work."

His speech was met with tepid applause. Diana clapped so she wouldn't arouse suspicion, but on the inside her head was spinning. She had to get to the Lane settlement and make sure Rick and his family were okay.

"Junior Agent Maple?"

Diana jumped in surprise. Mister Snow was standing right in front of her, with Benjamin at his side. "Yes, Mister Snow?"

"Job well done on the Lane problem. I'm very proud of you and Benjamin. I'm more proud of Benjamin, of course, but I recognize your contributions as well."

At that moment, Benjamin's face looked very punchable. Diana bit her lip so she wouldn't groan, uppercut him, or roll her eyes. "Thank you, sir."

"I have a special task for you both. It is more important than this celebration, so finish your extravagant beverages and follow me down to the vault."

The cave system ran deep into the continent. As the trio

traveled down, the sounds of far-off drilling echoed in their ears. Winterpole was already expanding the complex.

In the lower caverns was the water system. Winterpole had installed filtration pumps that poured millions of gallons of icy fresh water under the continent, chilling the region and providing drinking water for the agents. The water moved fast. Diana shivered as they crossed a narrow bridge over one of the rushing rivers.

At the very bottom of the complex, the walls had not been smoothed or polished yet; they were simply rough stone. Watching where they stepped on the slick rock floor, Mister Snow led the junior agents to a corridor. A caution sign hung over the opening to the corridor.

WARNING—UNDER CONSTRUCTION

Mister Snow removed the sign and went in. Diana and Benjamin followed. At the end of the corridor they came to a large circular door—the entrance to a vault.

"I didn't know this was here," Diana said.

Benjamin cast her a condescending glance. "Your impotent powers of observation will prevent you from advancing in Winterpole."

Good thing I don't want to advance in Winterpole, Diana thought to herself.

Mister Snow swiped a key card, twisted an old-fashioned copper key, and punched a code into a panel on the wall. A number of mechanisms popped at once.

There was a pneumatic hiss, and the vault door opened. Inside was a single sheet of cyber paper on an antique wooden table.

With the most delicate movements, Mister Snow picked up the cyber paper and showed it to Benjamin and Diana. "Winterpole created this document to be our contingency plan, in case the Lanes ever did acquire a certificate of occupancy. This is the Ultimate Continent Ownership Form."

"What is it?" Diana asked.

Mister Snow gave her a strange look. "It's the Ultimate Continent Ownership Form. I just said that."

"I mean, what does it *do*?"

"It allows a one-time activation. Whoever possesses the form when it's activated becomes the sole owner of the eighth continent. Thankfully the Lanes failed to get a certificate, and now we don't need to use it." Mister Snow closed the vault. It locked with another hiss. "The Ultimate Continent Ownership Form cannot be destroyed, so we must continue to guard it. That's where you two come in."

Diana looked at Benjamin and then back at Mister Snow. "Us?"

"Correct." Mister Snow handed Benjamin the key card, copper key, and a piece of paper with a password written on it. "You've done well. The ownership form is now your responsibility. In the event something happens to you, Junior Agent Maple will take over these duties. Remain vigilant, junior agents. I'm counting on you."

"Yes sir, Mister Snow!" Benjamin saluted.

Diana stared at the items in the boy's hand. If Rick and his family could get their hands on the ownership form, they still had a chance to control the continent. But that was a big if. The settlement had been destroyed. Diana wasn't even sure if the Lanes were still alive.

RICK COUGHED. HE OPENED HIS EYES, BUT ALL HE SAW WAS DARKNESS. HE COULD TELL HE WAS laying chest up, so he tried to maintain slow and steady breathing and let his vision adjust. His arms were pinned to his sides. He struggled. He felt beat up, sore all over, and the skin on his back was tender. Somehow, he managed to shove something heavy out of the way and raised his hands.

He continued to push, widening the tiny holes in whatever was covering him, and eventually broke free. Rick was standing among the wreckage of the smashed robo-giraffe walker. The explosion must have thrown him clear of the vehicle, but then the rubble landed on top of him. A heavy dome of plastic had absorbed most of the weight of the debris. He'd survived just by random chance.

The rest of the Lane settlement was leveled. Many of the hollow trees still burned. Spire One and Spire Two had collapsed, and splinters of fallen wood covered the ground like autumn leaves.

"Mom! Dad! Sprout!" Rick called out, but it hurt his back to shout. Nervously, he pulled up his T-shirt. He didn't even have to look. He could feel the burns on both shoulder blades, as well as his lower back. He should have figured— no one got out of an explosion like that scratch-free.

Some of the settlers wandered the devastation, looking for loved ones, seeing what they could salvage. When they saw Rick, they rushed over to check on him.

"I'm fine, it's okay," he assured them. "Go find whoever needs help. I need to look for my parents."

Over by the stump that had been Spire Two, Sprout was inspecting the broken entry doors and scratching his head. "Sprout! Thank the cosmos you're all right."

"Rick!" Sprout's face lit up. "Aw, boy, am I happy to see you. I need your help. I think there are some people trapped in the root system of Spire Two."

"Under the stump? Oh, dear! We have to get them out." Rick reached for the doors, but they were jammed.

"That's the problem," Sprout explained. "I can't seem to get inside."

"What about your lasso?" Rick asked. "Let's climb up and over."

"Hoo-wee! Good thinking, Rick." Sprout pulled out his looped rope and tossed it around a broken spike of wood above the door. He climbed the rope and quickly was over the wall, inside the stump. Rick followed, grunting in pain as he went up the rope. Every motion sent agony through his back. His thoughts drifted back to his fight in the head of the giraffe. He couldn't believe Evie was working with Vesuvia, that she had attacked the continent. And the things she had said. Rick didn't know what to think. No one knew of Evie's involvement but him . . . and he didn't know how to say anything.

Sprout caught Rick as he landed inside the stump. Everything was covered in big splinters the size of kitchen knives. They hurried over to the stairs that led down into the root system. They opened the door and started to descend.

But they couldn't proceed. A cave-in blocked the passage. Rick started to panic. This was the hall that led to his father's lab. He pulled out his pocket tablet and dialed his dad's number. "Dad! Dad! Are you all right?"

Scratchy and faint, his father's voice came back. "Rick! Are you okay? Your mother and I are trapped in the lab with Professor Doran."

"Dad! I'm so sorry. That's terrible."

"I know! Professor Doran won't stop talking about fungus. He's going to bore us both to death!"

"George!" Rick could hear his mother chiding his father in the background. "Be serious!"

"Oh, okay," Dad said. "I'm just kidding. We're safe. But the door's blocked. Looks like a cave-in. We are trapped down here."

"Don't worry, Dad. I'll think of something. Then I'll have you all out of there in a flash." He ended the call. "Sprout, we need to get some of the workers to help us dig them out."

"Righto, Rick!" Sprout led the way back up to the surface. He grabbed a fire axe from an emergency storage locker near the entrance. "Stand back!" Sprout cautioned, and then chopped at the jammed door. Three swings, and it broke open. Rick and Sprout spilled onto the ground outside.

To Rick's surprise, a Winterpole shuttle had landed in the middle of the settlement while he'd been underground. A crowd had gathered around the hovership. Diana was unloading pallets of bottled water, first aid kits, and other emergency supplies. She bent down to hand a bottle of water to a little boy, and when she stood up she brushed her hair out of her face and looked at Rick. He froze. She ran. And before Rick could react she pounced on him like a kitten attacking a ball of string.

"You're alive!" She pulled him into a tight hug. "When I saw what happened I feared the worst."

"I . . . um . . ." Rick stood there while she hugged him. It hurt a lot where she touched his back, but it still felt good somehow, so he just grimaced and kept quiet.

At last she pulled away and wiped her eyes. "Is everyone safe?"

"Some of us are hurt pretty bad," Rick explained. "And my parents are trapped in some of the wreckage. But everyone's alive."

"How can I help?" Diana asked, looking very serious.

"You've already done so much." Rick gestured to the supplies she had brought. "But honestly, I don't know what else you can do. The settlement has been destroyed. We've lost everything. And there's no way we're going to get the certificate of occupancy now."

"Actually . . ." Diana showed him a faint smile. "I may be able to help you with that."

Rick listened carefully as Diana described the Ultimate Continent Ownership Form that Benjamin was guarding back at the Winterpole base.

Adjusting his glasses, Rick said, "I don't know what's more distressing, that Winterpole has such a document in their possession, or that they've started their own society right here on the eighth continent."

Diana kicked some of the wood chips underfoot. "Honestly, even like this your settlement is cooler than what Winterpole has set up."

"Will you take me there? That ownership form may be our only hope of saving the continent."

"In a heartbeat," Diana said. "But it won't be easy to get past Benjamin, and Mister Snow isn't letting anything by him these days."

Rick scratched his chin. "All of my cyber paper was in my room in Spire One. So I have no permission slips at all. I'm defenseless."

"I may have a few documents on my shuttle," Diana replied. "And if we sneak you in, hopefully we won't need to use any of that stuff."

Turning to his other friend, Rick said, "Sprout, I have a big favor to ask you."

"Well, shoot, Rick. You know I'd do anything for you."

"I need you to lead the operation to dig my parents and Professor Doran out of the lab. Diana and I are going to pay a visit to Winterpole. Please, you need to stay behind and save them. I'm counting on you."

Humbly, Sprout removed his hat and covered his heart with it. "I will not fail."

"Thanks, buddy. I knew I could count on you."

"Follow me," Diana urged, leading Rick to her shuttle. "We have to hurry."

Each step toward the shuttle sent a shot of pain up Rick's back, but he didn't have time to rest or recover. These next few hours would decide the future of the continent he had come to call home. It was all up to him.

DIANA BROUGHT DOWN THE SHUTTLE A COUPLE OF MILES SOUTH OF THE WINTERPOLE COMPLEX.

The sun had gone to bed, and the forest was dark and quiet. She unbuckled and went to the shuttle's main hold to check on Rick.

He thumbed through a file folder of permission slips, pulled out a few choice pieces of cyber paper, and tucked them into a satchel. He fit the satchel over his shoulder and winced as the strap settled across his back.

"You're hurt," Diana said, coming up behind him.

"I'm fine," he assured her, but it sounded like a lie.

"Here . . ." She went to the storage hold and retrieved one last first aid kit. She pulled out a tube of ointment and wiggled it at him. "Let me see."

Grimacing, Rick turned and raised his shirt.

"Oh, gosh. These blisters look pretty bad."

"Sorry, I'm kind of scrawny," Rick apologized. "Not exactly the superhero we need right now."

Diana blushed. She smeared the ointment over his

131

injuries. The ointment was ice-cold and numbing. It made her fingers tingle. "It doesn't take muscles to make a hero, Rick. You're brave. That's what matters."

"It didn't feel very brave to run off, leaving my friends and family behind."

"You're looking at the bigger picture. Trying to save the continent."

"Yeah, but thinking about the big picture is what got me in this mess in the first place."

"What do you mean?" Diana finished applying the ointment to Rick's back. He lowered his shirt while she wiped her hands clean on a paper towel.

"I was so caught up with what I thought was best for the continent that I wasn't listening to what anyone else wanted. I chased Evie away. I abandoned her."

Diana didn't know what to say. She'd always thought Rick and Evie were very different, but that diversity made them stronger. She wished they could see that the way to succeed was to work together. If they pursued their own interests and never compromised, they'd be no better than Winterpole or Vesuvia.

"I was a pretty lousy big brother," Rick said, staring into the distance. "I get it now, why she ran away. So, yeah, Evie did something pretty dumb, but I forgive her. I just want her to come home."

"So let's go get her," Diana said. She wanted to do anything she could to help.

"She'll need a continent to come home to." Rick held his

satchel tight. "Let's get this ownership form, and then we'll find Evie."

They slipped noiselessly through the jungle. Diana guided him to a large gray rock beside a tree. The rock was vaguely shaped like an old TV set.

"Help me move this," Diana said, straining to pull the rock aside. Working together, they lifted the rock to reveal a tunnel leading down under the surface of the continent. Winterpole dug farther every hour. Unchecked, they would form a vast network of caverns under the whole continent.

As they moved down the tunnel, Diana gave Rick all the info she had. "The keys to the vault are in the possession of Benjamin Nagg, one of the other junior agents."

"Oh, yeah, you told me about him. Short kid, nasty attitude, loves nothing but himself?"

"That's Benjamin. This time of night he's probably gazing longingly into a bathroom mirror, flattering himself."

But as they searched the corridors of the Winterpole cavern system, they heard a voice echoing off the stones.

"I'm working as fast as I can. I'm onto something big. Just give me a little more time."

"That's Benjamin," Diana whispered.

"Who's he talking to?" Rick asked.

"I don't know." She strained to listen, but the other voice was garbled. It sounded like it was coming out of a phone.

"Fine!" Benjamin snapped. "Goodbye!"

They heard footsteps coming toward them.

Panicking, Diana looked around for a place to hide.

Rick calmly withdrew a piece of cyber paper from his bag. She hid behind him, hoping she wouldn't be seen.

Benjamin rounded the corner and froze. "Hey, aren't you—?"

"REDACTED!" Rick shouted, holding up the cyber paper. The document flashed blindingly white. Benjamin screamed and covered his eyes, doubling over in pain. Rick rushed over to him, rolling up the cyber paper.

"Do you have a way to knock him out?" Diana asked over Benjamin's loud groans.

"Kind of," Rick said, and then whacked Benjamin over the head with the cyberpaper. The weasely boy dropped to the floor and was out cold.

Diana stifled a laugh. "Aha. I see what you mean."

Rick put away the cyber paper. "Please don't tell my mom I did that."

They searched through Benjamin's pockets and found the key card, the copper key, and the password.

Squinting at the piece of paper, Rick read, "W-I-N-T-E-R-P-O-L-E-ONE-TWO-THREE? What are these guys, morons?"

"Don't dawdle," Diana warned. "Follow me."

They left Benjamin on the floor, and Diana led the way deeper into the tunnel system. After a winding journey, they arrived at the door to the vault.

"This is it," Diana said, looking around, feeling like Mister Snow was going to jump out of nowhere and lock them both up.

Rick moved to the door and swiped the key card, then

turned the lock with the copper key. He punched in the password and stepped back.

The door opened with a hiss. But there was no table. Since Diana had last looked inside the vault, a long tunnel had been dug beyond the vault door. It led down into darkness.

The Ultimate Continent Ownership Form was gone.

"Where did it go?" Diana asked, utterly confused.

"Your friend Benjamin probably wanted better security for the ownership form. So he built a second vault, deep inside the first one."

"Well, that's annoying," Diana said.

"Just a bit of a hiccup. Don't worry. I'll find it." Rick pocketed the key card, the copper key, and the scrap of paper and stepped through the open doorway.

"Right." Diana clapped her hands together. "Let's go."

"I'm sorry, Diana." Rick blocked the doorway. "It could be dangerous down there. And you've put yourself at enough risk already. No one from Winterpole can find out you're helping me. You have to maintain your cover."

"But Rick, I—"

"I'm sorry." He closed the door, sealing her out of the vault.

"Rick!" She grabbed the door, trying to pull it open, but it was no use. The lock had reset. She sighed, pressing her head against the cold metal of the vault door. "Good luck."

**EVIE SAT IN HER CELL AND WAITED. SHE WASN'T
SURE HOW MUCH TIME HAD PASSED SINCE THE**
guards had returned her to the prison, but her stomach
ached with hunger and her throat was sore. At some point,
she must have fallen asleep, but a deep rumbling that shook
the whole dreadnought had begun a couple of hours earlier,
and since then, she'd been wide awake.

From the slab in the corner of her cell, Evie could hear
footsteps at the far end of the hall, like the clanging of
someone wearing toasters for shoes. She went to the bars
and waited as 2-Tor and Didi appeared.

Didi stood stiffly as she greeted Evie. "Mrs. Piffle requests your presence on the bridge. There is something she
would like you to see before she disposes of you."

Evie looked to 2-Tor. "So now you're on Mastercorp's side?"

"I am on the side of my paramour, Miss Didi," 2-Tor
replied. "I have argued on your behalf, but to no avail. I am
sorry, Miss Evelyn. Truly, I am."

"That's it, then." Evie shrugged. "So hurry it up."

Didi opened the cell doors, and they escorted her from the prison. Evie walked quietly, head down, despondent. She deserved to be punished. She just hated that at the end she was going to be alone and facing someone as petty and vile as Viola Piffle. Back in the day, Dad had outsmarted Mastercorp. But Evie wasn't her father, that was certain.

A few minutes later, in one of the dark, winding halls of the dreadnought, 2-Tor stopped short. "I say, oh, dear. I seem to be jammed." His wings seized in an awkward pose, blocking most of the hallway.

"I just oiled you," Didi complained, grabbing at his wings, trying to move them.

"I do not have the foggiest idea what is causing this." 2-Tor sounded befuddled. He started backing up, little quick steps, bumping into Didi.

"Hey, bird brain! Be careful!" Didi swatted him on the head with a wing, but he kept moving back and stepped on one of her talons. They tripped and toppled over. 2-Tor pinned Didi to the ground as he flailed and flopped around. "I say! This is most irregular!"

"Get off!" Didi screamed.

2-Tor flapped his wings at Evie. "Run, Evelyn! Hurry! Go!"

Evie didn't stop to think or ask questions, she just ran. She ducked around a corner, not looking back. On the inside her heart was soaring. 2-Tor had risked everything for the chance to save her. She felt so foolish for doubting him.

Signs hung on the walls at some intersections, but the

labyrinthine dreadnought was still nearly impossible to navigate. Evie ran aimlessly, trying to find her way back to the docking bay and the exit. She had to escape over the bridge that led to New Miami. From there, she could escape into the woods, and then . . . she wasn't sure, but she didn't have time to think about it now.

Evie skidded to a stop as she came upon a catwalk that crossed a deep chasm. In the middle of the pit, rising up past the catwalk, was a communications tower. She had seen Rick set up a similar but much smaller device back at the settlement. She reasoned that all communications from the dreadnought must be routed out through this tower.

Rick. In case Evie didn't make it out of the dreadnought, she had to let Rick know that Mastercorp was on the continent. She had to let him know how sorry she was.

Evie ventured across the wobbly catwalk, trying not to look down. When she reached the communications tower, she quickly opened up their systems. Her computer skills were a little rusty, but she managed to get a feed to Rick's pocket tablet. For some reason he didn't pick up, but that was probably for the best. She didn't think she was ready to face him.

Taking a deep breath, Evie looked into the camera and left her message.

When she finished, she closed the feed and hurried to the other side of the catwalk. Soon she found a sign with directions to the docking bay. *At last!* she thought.

The docking bay was strangely deserted. The hoverships

were all there, but the mechanics, soldiers, and guards who were always bustling around the staging area were nowhere to be seen. At the far end of the docking bay, the jagged mouth of the black robo-shark was closed tightly. Evie flipped the lever that extended the bridge out of the shark's mouth and hurried across as the great black maw yawned open. Wind blasted through the open portal, whipping her hair as she ran.

Her hopes fell when she reached the end of the bridge and could see outside the mouth. Now that incessant rumbling made sense. At some point during the night, the dreadnought had taken off and was now flying over New Miami. The bridge extended to nowhere and dead-ended at a thousand-foot drop to the ocean below.

Evie searched for another way out. Maybe she could steal a hovership and fly to safety.

"Caw! Caw!" Something black swooped past her head. She ducked out of the way. It was a black raven, a model of metal robo-bird she had never seen before. It flew around in a tight arc and dove at Evie again. She screamed as it flew by, slicing a gash in her arm with a razor-sharp wing.

More birds flapped toward her. "Rawwk! Caw!"

Evie shielded her face with her arms and ran back up the bridge, trying to avoid the deadly flying robots. The birds perched on her head and shoulders. She tried to shoo them away, but they pecked at her, sending stabbing pains through her body.

The birds grabbed Evie with their beaks and talons and

flapped their wings, pulling her into the air. She kicked and struggled, but it was no use. They carried her back to the black metal floor of the docking bay and dropped her hard. She landed on her knees.

Viola Piffle stood before her, tall and imposing. She smoothed her blond hair flat against her head as one of the ravens landed on her shoulder, glaring at Evie with eyes that glowed like hot coals.

"Come now, little Lane," Viola said as Evie struggled to get to her feet. "There is no escape for you."

RICK COULD HEAR DIANA'S PROTESTS THROUGH THE SEALED VAULT DOOR, BUT HE DIDN'T DARE

change his mind now. He had to protect her—she'd already done so much for him. He took the illumination request form from his satchel and switched it on, casting faint light down the tunnel. These forms had been designed to order lawyers to clarify their oft-baffling contract language—pretty smart to have the forms illuminate tunnels as well as ideas.

The ground was uneven, and Rick was grateful for the light. He stepped carefully, and after a few hundred feet he came to a small, square room with walls of stone. In the center of the room was a glass box on a wooden table. A piece of notebook paper was taped to the glass. It read:

> DO NOT TOUCH—seriously, if you touch this form I will flick your ear, and it won't feel good. I promise you won't like it. Then after I flick your ear I'll kill you, so seriously, HANDS OFF.
> —BENJAMIN NAGG

Rick crumpled the paper and tossed it aside, then carefully removed the glass case. There, lying flat and square on the table, like a place mat, was the Ultimate Continent Ownership Form. It looked so simple, so unambiguous, so unlike the other Winterpole documents he had studied. In fancy script, the piece of paper said, *"By every island and isthmus, by every archipelago, whosoever holds this document shall possess full ownership of THE 8TH CONTINENT."*

Rick shrugged and grabbed the paper off the table.

The blaring alarm that immediately sounded should not have surprised him. Stuffing the ownership form into his satchel, he ran back up the tunnel, hit the button next to the vault door to open it, and then ducked into the hallway. The alarm was loud—teeth-achingly loud—and Rick could barely hear himself think. Diana was nowhere in sight. When the alarm sounded she must have run off. *Good*, Rick thought.

He ran through the rocky tunnels, looking for a way out. He passed by the spot where they had encountered Benjamin, but the boy agent was gone. Rick kept going.

The next hallway opened onto an underground river. The water surged, cascading over rocks and flowing through the tunnels. Feeling a cool mist on his face, Rick looked around for a way to get across. He spotted a narrow metal bridge over his head. He climbed up the rock wall one story to the bridge. Before Rick could start across the river, he realized he had company.

Mister Snow stood on the bridge in a spotless white

suit, holding an old-fashioned briefcase in one hand. He straightened his tie and silently watched Rick with eyes like laser beams.

Rick opened his satchel and reached inside. His hand settled on the gag order he had brought with him. There was no chance he was going to let the Winterpole agent stop him. He took his first step onto the bridge. It wobbled a bit. The metal was wet and slippery.

"Get out of my way, Mister Snow. I'm leaving with the ownership form."

Only the agent's lips moved. "You always were the petulant one, Richard Lane. You always had to have your way. Just like your father."

"Don't make me hurt you," Rick said.

With the flick of the agent's finger, the briefcase popped open a few inches. Reams of cyber paper glowed inside. "I am not the slightest bit concerned about that, young man. You want to push paper with me? Go ahead and try."

"No talking!" Rick shouted, flinging the gag order across the bridge at Mister Snow. The small card of cyber paper flapped like a bird as it flew, but as it neared Mister Snow's face, the agent produced a sheet of cyber paper from his briefcase and swung it at Rick's gag order. "Cancel that command." He spoke as calmly as an airline pilot. The gag order fizzled and fell to the ground. The glow of the cyber paper faded. Mister Snow had used his cancel order form and returned it to the briefcase in one fluid motion, like an *iaido* master.

Rick had an excused absence sheet in his satchel. It would allow him to leave the complex unharmed. He reached into the satchel, but Mister Snow tore another sheet from his briefcase. "Privileges revoked!" There was a flash of yellow light. When Rick pulled at his excusal form, all the power had been drained from his cyber paper.

"Now you are mine, Richard Lane. You will be remanded to our headquarters in Geneva for interrogation. I'll make sure you're never given permission to return to the eighth continent again."

Rick grabbed a lockdown order, but Mister Snow retaliated with a stunning attack from a cyber sheet. The sonic blasts knocked Rick back against the rails.

"Give me the ownership form."

"Never!"

"Then I'll destroy it, along with you!"

Mister Snow flung an expulsion certificate at Rick's feet. It exploded, tearing a hole through the bridge and knocking Rick over the rails. He screamed as he fell. Mister Snow looked down at him, watching with a hardened glare.

The icy drink swallowed Rick, sweeping him under.

22

EVIE STRUGGLED AGAINST THE ROPES THAT BOUND HER WRISTS BEHIND HER BACK. NO ONE NOTICED her attempts to escape. The bridge of the dreadnought was a flurry of activity. Mister Dark directed the movements of the hover shark over New Miami, while Viola Piffle led a team of technicians in arming several bombs with a supply of the silvery Anti-Eden Compound. Her razor-winged birds watched the scene from perches near the ceiling all around the bridge. Their devilish faces made Evie miss the Piffle Pink Patrol, as crazy as that seemed to her.

Vesuvia stayed close to her mother, helping with the arming of the bomb, while Didi paced worriedly. 2-Tor sat beside Evie, his wings tied down against his sides.

"I'm sorry I got us into this mess," Evie whispered to 2-Tor. "This is all my fault. If I hadn't run off, you wouldn't have had to chase after me. You'd still be a real bird, and none of this would have happened."

"Nonsense, my dear girl," 2-Tor blubbered, his personality circuits going haywire. "I was taken in by a beguiling enemy and offered you unsound counsel. I promise if we get out of this scrape I will defend you to your family and anyone else, down to my last percent of battery."

"Thanks, 2-Tor," Evie sniffled, leaning against the bird's metal frame.

"There," Viola said with cold satisfaction, stepping away from her bomb and smoothing her hair against her head. "Assembly complete. The chairman will be thrilled with our success."

"The chairman is *never* thrilled," Mister Dark corrected. "But we have the Anti-Eden Compound. That's what matters."

"Yes, truly." With a wicked smile, Viola turned to Evie. "Your father's chemical discovery was monumental, but he chose to forget that in actuality it belonged to *us*. Now it has returned to its rightful owners and has been weaponized, as it was meant to be."

"You're monsters," Evie spat.

Viola shrugged dismissively. "You're getting ahead of yourself, my dear. Don't call us monsters until you witness us testing our superweapon. Speaking of which, I believe it's time for a practical demonstration. Prepare to drop the Anti-Eden bomb!"

Vesuvia said, "Mom, where should I tell them to direct the dreadnought?"

"Why, nowhere, you stupid girl." Viola patted the bomb like it was a prized cow. "All we need to test the bomb is a piece of the eighth continent. Our current location will suffice."

Looking very confused, Vesuvia stuttered, "But . . . New Miami is down there."

"Why, yes, of course, dear." Her mother laughed. "We couldn't very well test the power of the bomb on an uninhabited portion of the continent, could we? Besides, we have to destroy your oversized dollhouses if we're going to make room for our weapons factories."

"F-factories?"

Viola retched. "You really are dense. Dee-Two, haven't you taught my stupid daughter anything? Dee-Two?"

Didi suddenly jerked. She had been standing perfectly still, staring across the room at 2-Tor. "I am sorry, madame. Yes. My memory banks indicate successful education on a variety of topics."

Rolling her eyes, Viola said, "Will somebody set up this bomb, please?" The technicians ran to be the first to grab the bomb and start dragging it out of the bridge on a little dolly.

"NO!" Vesuvia shrieked. "Don't touch that. Nobody's going to destroy New Miami. Nobody is going to bomb anything unless *I say so!*"

"You really are foolish." Her mother shook her head. "This isn't the first bomb we are assembling. It's the last. Release the bombs, Mister Dark."

The viewscreens hanging around the bridge switched to images of the dreadnought and New Miami. Bomb bays opened on the base of the shark, and two bombs tumbled out. They landed in the middle of New Miami with a splash of silver liquid. Evie couldn't look away. The Anti-Eden Compound chewed through the earth, morphing it back into trash—rotten food, plastic bags, broken machinery. Without the sturdy foundation, buildings buckled and collapsed. A hotel landed on top of a juice bar. The ground underneath a surf shop melted into Styrofoam cups, and the whole store floated out to sea.

Vesuvia grabbed a chair and raised it over her head. "I said stop!" She swung hard, smashing the chair against the side of the bomb. "Don't bomb New Miami! Don't!" She struck the bomb again, putting a huge dent in the metal exterior.

"Vesuvia!" her mother shouted, aghast.

"Shut up, Mommy!" Vesuvia smashed the chair to pieces as she hit the bomb a third time, puncturing a hole in the metal shell. The hole started leaking silvery fluid.

"Uh . . . Vesuvia . . ." Evie cautioned. "Maybe you should take it easy."

"Don't tell me what to do, Peevy Evie!" Vesuvia went into full-on tantrum mode. She ran into the bomb at full speed. It wobbled on the rolling dolly and toppled over. Viola stepped out of the way. The technicians ran for cover. As the bomb struck the floor, the shell split open, and the Anti-Eden Compound poured across the dreadnought's bridge.

"2-Tor!" Evie screamed as the flood rushed toward them.

**COLD, WET SAND PRESSED AGAINST RICK'S FACE.
THAT WAS THE FIRST THING HE FELT AS HE WOKE**
up in the dim light of dawn. He could feel water rushing
over his feet. His arm underneath him had fallen asleep.
Droplets of water covered his glasses, and his hair was
soaking wet. The memory of his duel with Mister Snow
returned—the embarrassing memory of getting his butt
packaged in a petite box, wrapped in tinsel, and offered to
him as a gift.

At least he was in one piece. He tried to get up. Pain
punched him in a dozen places from his forehead down to
his toes. The burns on his back stung like hornets. He decided to stay put for a moment.

A foot away from his face, Rick's pocket tablet lay
half-embedded in the sand. *ONE UNVIEWED MESSAGE* was
blinking at him on the screen. He reached over, wiped some
sand off the screen, and tapped on the message.

Evie's face appeared. She looked worried and out of
breath, her head surrounded by darkness. "Rick . . . I'm sorry.

I did a stupid thing. I wish I could take it all back, everything I did. But I can't. I'm being held captive by Vesuvia's mother on the west coast of the continent. She works for Mastercorp. I'm trying to escape, but this place is heavily guarded, and I don't know if I'll make it. If you don't hear from me . . . please . . . come find me. I need your help. Rick . . . I—"

A black boot came down and crushed the pocket tablet, shattering the screen, and Evie's image, into a hundred triangles.

Rick tried to look up at the person standing over him. He crouched down and, with a snap of his finger, flicked Rick's ear.

"Ow!" Rick said.

"Shut up." Benjamin flicked Rick's ear again. "Didn't you read my note? You should learn not to touch other people's stuff."

"How did you—"

Benjamin hopped up and kicked Rick hard in the stomach. Rick gasped as his air left him. He curled up, choking on his own throat.

"Tsk, tsk, Lane. The smart move would have been to drown when Mister Snow threw you in the river. Now you have to deal with me."

Rick had to find a way to get out of this. Evie was in trouble. She needed his help. He had to get to her before Mastercorp did anything to her, or before Benjamin did anything else to him.

"Give it to me," Benjamin ordered, turning Rick over. He had a nasty, determined look on his face. "Give me that ownership form."

Rick grunted as Benjamin tore away his satchel and dug through it. He pulled out the Ultimate Continent Ownership Form and held it up triumphantly. "Aha! Here you are, my beauty." He stuffed the form into his pocket, looking satisfied, and threw the satchel in the river. It sank below the surface and was carried downstream, between some trees.

While Benjamin gloated, Rick tried to crawl away. Benjamin stepped on his foot, pinning him. "Ah, ah, ah! Not so fast, Lane. I haven't figured out what I'm going to do with you yet."

Clawing at the sand, Rick said, "Winterpole policy states that you need to return me unharmed to the nearest senior agent for interrogation."

Benjamin grabbed Rick's shoulders and pulled him to his feet. The boy was surprisingly strong for his diminutive size, and when he dug his fingers into Rick's blistering skin, the pain felt like he was being burned all over again. "And what makes you think I care about Winterpole policy?"

Rick hesitated. "Uhh . . . because you're a Winterpole agent? Because you . . ." He trailed off. Benjamin was smirking, and that grin twisted into the most demonic expression Rick had ever seen.

"You understand now," Benjamin said plainly.

"You're a double agent. You don't work for Winterpole. You work for Mastercorp."

"That's right, Ricky! You can't imagine how painful it has been for me to put up with all their stupid rules and ancient technology. And the food is the blandest cardboard I've ever tasted. I cannot wait until we destroy Winterpole, and Mastercorp takes over as the world's primary rule-making organization. Privatization! It's the way of the future! Now come with me. It's time for you to meet my boss."

Benjamin pulled Rick into a grove of trees, where his hovership was parked. He chained Rick to one of the seats in the cockpit and took off. Soon, they were flying west across the continent. Benjamin thought he had achieved a great victory, but unbeknownst to him, west, to Mastercorp, was exactly where Rick wanted to go.

WHEN DIANA ENTERED MISTER SNOW'S OFFICE, HE WAS STANDING IN THE CORNER BY THE FILING

cabinet, sorting cyber paper documents. "What is it, Junior Agent?"

She tried to collect her thoughts. She had known exactly what she wanted to say when she walked in the room, but now that she was here, all those great ideas had left her. "I, well, you see . . ."

"Spit it out, Maple." Mister Snow slammed the filing cabinet shut and returned to the high-backed chair behind his desk, which was completely empty except for a typewriter and two number two pencils.

"I think we've been making a huge mistake about the Lanes."

"The Lane family is a menace," Mister Snow explained. "We've been dealing with their troublemaking for years."

"But what exactly have they done? Rescued a few birds from endangered habitats? Transformed the Great Pacific

Garbage Patch into the continent we're standing on right now? I'd like to file this request form with you, sir."

Mister Snow picked up the paper she slid across the desk. "And what's this?"

"A formal request for you to give me a break, sir." Diana was thoroughly expecting him to throw her out and possibly lock her up for insubordination, so there was no point in going halfway. "Mastercorp is the real problem. Polluting the earth, manufacturing weapons that are hard to regulate."

"Winterpole gives Mastercorp a pass because of the alliance your own mother negotiated," Mister Snow said. "Do you realize you're going against her by saying such treasonous things?"

Diana swallowed. "I do realize this, sir, and I actually think the Lane family would make exceptional leaders of the continent."

"Better than us?!" Mister Snow asked, sounding appalled.

"We're rule enforcers," Diana replied. "We are exceptional at that. But someone else should be the rule makers, don't you think?"

"I've been after George Lane for years. And ever since his pesky kids got in the mix, it's been harder. Too hard!" Mister Snow's face grew red as he spoke.

"Rick and Evie fought to destroy the Great Pacific Garbage Patch," Diana countered. "I can't even imagine how much pollution they eradicated. It was a great deed. We owe them some credit for doing our job for us. They are keeping the planet safe and clean."

Mister Snow scowled. "Reports have been flooding Winterpole Headquarters that Mastercorp has been damaging habitats on all *eight* continents."

"So don't you think it's time to change agency policy?" Diana asked.

Mister Snow glared at her. She crossed her fingers and waited for him to speak.

EVIE SCRABBLED AWAY FROM THE ANTI-EDEN COMPOUND AS IT OOZED TOWARD HER. IN THE commotion, the pilot of the hovership slipped, and the dreadnought veered. Everyone stumbled around the bridge, trying to stay clear of the deadly compound. It seeped through cracks in the floor panels, dripping down into the rest of the ship.

Mrs. Piffle swung at her daughter. "You idiot! Look what you've done, you spoiled brat."

"I hate you!" Vesuvia screamed, totally apathetic to the crisis on the bridge. "You lied to me! This was never part of the deal."

"Contain her, Mrs. Piffle!" Mister Dark ordered. "Or I will do it for you."

"Be careful, Evelyn." 2-Tor struggled to his feet, straining against his bonds.

Evie pulled away as the Anti-Eden Compound came closer. She didn't know what would happen if she touched the compound, but she didn't want to find out. Then she got an idea. The rope tying her hands was made of plant fibers, and the Anti-Eden Compound altered organic materials. Careful not to touch any herself, Evie turned around and dipped the rope into the liquid. The chemical reaction was immediate, turning the rope into brittle strands of a tinfoil-like material. She broke free and grabbed 2-Tor, quickly undoing his restraints.

"Let's go, bird. Run!"

They fled the bridge, not waiting to see what became of Vesuvia or the dripping compound. As they left, Didi waved goodbye. "Farewell, my darling Toots! Farewell! I will never forget you!"

They went down the first staircase they found. They had to get to the docking bay and off the dreadnought before the leaking Anti-Eden Compound dripped on them.

When they reached the docking bay, a small Winterpole shuttle was coming in for a landing. It touched down, and the hatch opened. A pale, skinny boy with slick black hair emerged. He had Rick with him, in handcuffs.

"Rick!" Evie ran to them. "What are you doing here?"

"I came here to rescue you," Rick explained as the other boy reached for the icetinguisher on his belt.

"Waaark!" 2-Tor leaped forward, knocking the boy to the ground. The icetinguisher slid across the floor. "No one is going to bother my children any more today!"

"2-Tor!" Rick stared in disbelief. "What happened to you?"

The bird looked down at his metal body. "Believe me when I confess it is a very long story."

"Yup! Time for that later," Evie said. "We gotta get out of here."

"Great." Rick held up the handcuffs. "The keys to these are on Benjamin's shuttle. We can take that to get home."

"Good idea," Evie said, leading him and 2-Tor aboard. While 2-Tor found the key and freed Rick, Evie powered up the engine and took off. She flew toward the dreadnought's open mouth.

"You can't escape, Lanes!" Benjamin was hanging from the hovership's entry door, icetinguisher in hand.

"Man, this dude is persistent," Evie complained, rocking the ship side to side to try to shake him off. But Benjamin grabbed hold of the door handle and climbed aboard.

"Evie, look out!" Rick cried, shoving Benjamin as he fired his weapon. Evie dodged the blast, but it struck the pilot's console, freezing the controls.

The hovership careened out of the dreadnought and tumbled down, toward the surface. The four passengers flew around the spiraling cockpit. Evie fell against the console. It stung her hands to touch the frozen controls. She punched the flight wheel, trying to shatter the chemically formed ice locking it in place. *Crack.* She hit the wheel again. *Crack.* Through the viewport, the ground was coming up fast.

Smash! On the third hit, the ice shattered, and Evie pulled up on the controls as hard as she could. The others dropped to the floor as the hovership leveled off. But it was coming in too fast. The hovership slammed into the main boulevard, but the rapidly deteriorating rock cushioned their fall.

Smoke billowed from the wrecked console. While Benjamin struggled to his feet, Evie helped Rick and 2-Tor up, and they escaped the hovership.

People fled New Miami in a panic. Streams of Anti-Eden Compound flowed through the streets. Careful not to step in the silver puddles, Evie led the way across the city.

"Come on, children," 2-Tor instructed. "Hold on to me. I will whisk us out of here with a quick flight."

Rick and Evie grabbed 2-Tor around the middle. The bird raised his metal wings and prepared for liftoff.

"LANES!!!" roared Benjamin. He aimed his icetinguisher and fired another blast. The blue goop spattered 2-Tor's wings, freezing them into brittle slabs.

"I say, it appears I am stuck."

"Unflappable as usual, 2-Tor. Now come on, run!" Evie sprinted across the wobbly terrain.

Benjamin pulled the trigger again. *Click*. He was out of freeze gel. He tossed the weapon aside and gave chase.

At the edge of the city, one of the bombs had shot a geyser of Anti-Eden Compound sideways, forming a river that cut a deep ravine with slopes of garbage up either side.

"We have to get across," Rick said.

"Okay, we'll jump." Evie ran down the slope of the ravine, hopping from garbage bag to garbage bag like they were stepping-stones. Rick and 2-Tor followed her across, the latter looking quite silly with his frozen blue wings jutting out of him.

The ground rumbled. Evie's foot sank into the dirt, which had turned to the consistency of marshmallows. She saw moldy bread and broken lightbulbs and, yes, even half-eaten marshmallows. Rick grabbed her and pulled her free, like plucking a big carrot from the earth. "I got you," he said. "You're okay."

"Lanes, help!" Benjamin was trapped, standing on a bag of trash while the river of Anti-Eden Compound split on either side of him.

He was a huge jerk, but Evie couldn't just leave him exposed to the Anti-Eden Compound. After seeing its effects, she wouldn't wish that fate on anybody. From the far bank, she crept down to the river's edge. "I'm coming!" she said.

Upstream, the bomb burst, pouring a wave of Anti-Eden Compound into the river. With a roar of sound, the wave overtook Benjamin, engulfed him, and swept him away.

"Whoa," Evie gasped, horrified. But then, *squish*, her foot sank into the ground again.

"Evie!" Rick cried, running down the bank to save her.

"Wait, Rick, don't come!" But it was too late. The ground all around them had turned into a roiling pool of trash, and Rick sank up to his waist. He reached out for Evie. She grabbed his hand, but as they pulled they only managed to sink deeper. The garbage was almost up to their shoulders.

"Children!" 2-Tor squawked. "Do not despair! I shall waddle for help at the speediest of clips." The ground beneath

2-Tor's feet gave out, and he sank as well, surrounded by balled-up plastic grocery bags. "*Waark!* Foiled by pollution!"

They didn't have much time left. The eighth continent had been garbage before the Eden Compound transformed it, and now it was garbage once again. Sinking into a vast sea of smelly trash seemed like a pretty terrible end to their adventure, but if these minutes were to be their last, Evie wanted to set things right.

"Rick, I'm so sorry. I ruined everything."

Under the surface of the trash soup, Rick found her hands and squeezed them tightly. "No, Evie, it was my fault. I shouldn't have pushed you away. I didn't trust you when I should have. I'm no good as a leader without you. We need to work together."

Evie looked around at the garbage that had risen up to their necks. "Yeah, sure . . . I'll make a mental note of that and jot it down in my self-improvement journal."

Rick raised his chin so it wouldn't touch the grime. "I'm serious, Evie, if we get out of this mess, we can't let the continent be a dictatorship. We need to serve the people of this continent together, Evie. As a team."

"I thought you hated me."

"Hated you? I came all the way here to rescue you. But then I was the one who needed rescuing. Thanks for that, by the way."

"Sure, no problem. Glad I could save you." Evie grimaced. This was it. One more breath, and then she'd be under the surface.

"I love you, sis."

"I love you too, bro!"

Evie closed her eyes and waited for the inevitable.

"Yeehaw! There them smelly varmints are!"

Above their heads, a tree and a silver bird swooped across the sky. It was Mom and Dad in the *Condor*, and Sprout and Professor Doran in the *Roost*. Their parents went after the dreadnought, chasing the big Mastercorp shark away from the coast, while their beloved tree flew low and dropped a vacuum, slurping up Evie, Rick, and 2-Tor.

"Ugggccccch . . ." Evie groaned as she landed on the deck of the storage hold. "That smell is like Gorgonzola cheese cosplaying as a sewer."

Rick gagged. "It's like a skunk brushed its teeth with brown guacamole."

Evie would have retched at Rick's description if she hadn't already been retching at the smell. She couldn't help but laugh.

"Hoo-wee!" Sprout fanned the stench away with his cowboy hat as he arrived in the storage hold. "Y'all smell worse than a desert outhouse."

Together, Rick and Evie said, "We know!"

26

THE CELL DOORS SLAMMED SHUT WITH A HUMBLING CLANG. VESUVIA DROPPED TO THE FLOOR OF THE barren room, wailing in misery. "Why are you putting me in here?! There isn't even a bed. Just this horrible slab. It's cruel, I tell you. Let me out!"

Vesuvia's mother did not look like she was about to listen to her daughter's protestations. Her face was a tapestry of disappointment and disgust. "You betrayed us. You ruined our plan. You've cost Mastercorp millions. Formal charges will be filed against you in short order. In the meantime, enjoy your probation."

"Mommy . . . please!" Vesuvia begged.

"Don't call me that," the woman said. She smoothed her hair against her head and left.

27

BACK AT THE LANE SETTLEMENT, RICK AND EVIE RUSHED TO THEIR PARENTS' ARMS AS SOON AS they disembarked from the *Condor*. Through all the happy tears of joy and relief, Evie babbled, "Mom, Dad, I'm so sorry. I don't know what I was thinking. I ruined everything."

"Nonsense, my darling dear." Dad patted her on the head. "We've got lots to fix up, and you're going to have more work to do than anyone, but we'll be better too."

"That's right!" Mom agreed. "We'll listen. You deserve to have a say in things. And we'll make this continent the best one ever."

Rick squeezed into the family hug. At last, they were back together. And although there was much to do before things were normal again (or at least the Lanes' wacky definition of normal), Evie was home safe.

A loud rustling of trees drew their attention to the edge of the jungle. Large crowds of refugees were arriving from the destroyed New Miami. The Lanes would need to rebuild, all right, bigger and better than before.

Sprout and Professor Doran happily reported that the re-construction process had already begun. More hollow-tree seeds were being transferred to the eighth continent from the professor's farm. The settlers were hard at work clean-ing what remained of the old settlement and adding new structures. They may have failed to acquire the certificate of occupancy, and Rick may have lost the Ultimate Continent Ownership Form, but that wasn't going to stop them from building the paradise of their dreams. Even if it wouldn't be a society where everyone was free to come and live, at least they would be together as a family.

But a non-Lane had taken over the struggling settle-ment in their absence, a shade-wearing, beat-dropping, bass-thumping maniac by the name of Tristan Ruby. When the settlers took breaks from their work, they would crowd around the portable DJ station Tristan had set up and dance to his music.

"Who's this weirdo?" Evie asked, inspecting the scene.

Rick explained all the trouble he'd had with the party planner while Evie was away. "He's the absolute worst. I haven't been able to get him to follow orders. Maybe you know how to put a stop to his troublemaking."

Evie dusted off her hands and walked closer. "Never fear, Ricky-poo, I'm on it."

Tristan raised his glasses to get a better look at Evie. "Well, hey! Look at that. A little dudette."

Evie planted her feet and shook her hips, waving her arms in the air, dancing madly. Rick covered his face, embarrassed.

"Cool jams!" Evie said, dancing closer to Tristan. "I love this."

"Aww, thanks, little dudette. Happy to cheer you up. Nice moves."

"I do my best! So listen, a huge island of trash is floating off the west coast that used to be New Miami. Rick thinks the eighth continent may have lost more than ten percent of its total land area. We have to mount a massive cleanup effort pronto. Plus, there's a lot of work to do on the settlement, so workers are going to need to stay focused on that. We should cool it with the dance parties for a while."

"Sorry, the party can't ever stop."

"But *everyone* is going to need to chip in, even you, mister."

"No kidding?" Tristan raised his eyebrows over the rims of his glasses.

"Not even a little bit."

"But my music can't be held back."

Evie smiled. "You'll still get to host your parties. It'll be great for keeping morale up, but no more late-night dancefests. We have to stay focused on the important tasks at hand."

"No way. I don't need any of your silly rules. My peeps gotta cut loose!" Tristan responded.

Evie nodded like an enlightened martial arts master. Something about her was different, and Rick liked it. "You say you don't need our rules, but if you don't participate, then you can't get any of the benefits our settlement provides."

"Don't need none of those, neither!" Tristan said.

"Oh really? When your sound system runs out of juice, you recharge your batteries with our generators. You eat our food, you sleep in our shelters. You host your dance parties in the buildings we built. I'd say you need plenty of the things we provide."

"Yeah, but . . . well, I . . ."

"That's what I thought." Evie grinned victoriously. "Work with us, and we'll make sure you have rocking dance parties for a long, long time."

Tristan Ruby extended his hand. "Nice to meet you, little dudette. Welcome home."

Returning to the crowd of family members, Evie winked at her brother. "See? Easy as asking nicely."

The deep, loud horn of a dump truck promptly ended their conversation. The hefty vehicle rumbled through the jungle, squeezed between two big trees, and parked in front of Rick and Evie. The back of the dump truck was filled with more paperwork than Rick had ever seen.

Diana hopped out of the cab of the truck and rushed over to her friends. "Hi, everyone! I have a surprise for you."

She turned back to the truck, and Mister Snow stepped down from the driver's side.

Everyone got tense. Mister Snow had put Dad away at the Prison at the Pole. Rick was still sore from his cyber paper battle at the Winterpole complex.

"Hello . . ." Mister Snow said with an awkward wave. In the warm sunlight, he looked full of starch in his glacier-white suit. "Greetings, fellow citizens of the eighth continent."

"Diana, what are you doing?" Rick asked worriedly. "Why is he here?"

"Why?" Mister Snow's mouth curled into a sneer. "I'm here because I have temporarily suspended my sizable reservations and considerable dislike for you and your family. Junior Agent Maple has made a compelling case for your continued inhabitance of this fledgling continent. After careful consideration, in concordance with my duties as Senior Winterpole Official in Charge of the Eighth Continent, I have deemed the Lane settlement fit for a certificate of occupancy."

"What?!" Rick asked in disbelief.

Evie hung on his arm. "You're serious?"

"As serious as a slippery floor with inadequate caution signage, young lady. But with a few provisos. Please see the attached four-million-page document." Mister Snow gestured toward the mountain of paperwork in the back of the truck. "The important thing is that you may start inviting new citizens to come right away. Winterpole will be present to monitor your progress and ensure that everything you do comes with the appropriate permission slip. Miss Maple has volunteered to be your permanent liaison. She's one of our most promising young agents. I don't envy you, having a stickler like her around."

Rick stifled a laugh as Diana flashed him the least subtle wink he had ever seen.

Mister Snow adjusted his tie. "There's one other caveat that is not mentioned in any of the paperwork."

"Are you sure?" Evie asked, inspecting the overflowing truck bed. "Because it looks like pretty much everything is mentioned in there."

Ignoring her, Mister Snow said, "We have to deal with our mutual adversary. Mastercorp is in gross violation of Winterpole statutes, constructing weapon-manufacturing facilities in unmonitored territory. Once they repair the damages to their dreadnought, they will return for more devious activities. We may call upon Lane Industries to help us put a stop to them."

"Of course! Anything we can do to help!" Dad said with a big grin, extending his hand.

Mister Snow hesitated. Diana nudged him. He leaned forward and graciously shook the hand of his old nemesis.

The deal was sealed. Rick was elated. He had his home. He had his family. And for the moment, he had the greatest thing any of them could have asked for. Peace.

CONSCIOUSNESS REGAINED. OUTSIDE STIMULI OVERWHELMING SENSORS. REDUCING OPTICS, SONAR, AND TACTILE RECEPTORS TO TWENTY-FIVE PERCENT. ADJUST APERTURE. SIT UP. SIT UP. SIT UP.

Benjamin lurched. His mission was a failure. The Lanes had escaped.

Mastercorp had left him behind, left him to die, drown in the filth and trash that surrounded him, the wrecked ruins of New Miami. He swore he would get his revenge on them, just as soon as he got his revenge on the Lanes.

Why did he feel so heavy? He could barely move. He could barely see—just a silvery blur in front of his eyes. He moved away from where he'd woken up, lumbering like Frankenstein's monster. As his vision cleared, he discovered he was at the edge of a river of Anti-Eden Compound, near the shore.

New Miami had disintegrated into trash. Returned to its original state, this large island of the Great Pacific

Garbage Patch had drifted offshore. The rest of the continent remained the tropical paradise it had become.

Benjamin reached the water and knelt down.

AQUATIC HAZARD DETECTED. DEPLOY HYDRO-PHOBIC SEALANT.

What was that? A voice in his head? Benjamin winced. It felt like the voice was shouting directly into his ear. And then he felt this pressure all through his body. Shaking it off, he dipped his hands into the water—he wanted to splash water on his face.

Benjamin stopped short. Gauntlets. He was wearing silver gauntlets. They were thick metal with clawed fingertips, nasty things. He could stab straight through a side of meat with these. But hold that thought. First, water.

He splashed the water on his face. *KA-DONG!*

Benjamin froze. He caressed his cheeks and nose. Something didn't feel right, even with the gauntlets. Crawling on his hands and knees, he splashed into the water and waited for the ripples to settle. He stared at his reflection. That face. That metal, lifeless face. Like a silver skull, with eyes like agonized lava.

He punched the metal face with his claws. Nothing would dent it. The sharp scraping thuds pounded his aural sensors. He looked himself over. His whole body had transformed. He was a monster, a hideous freak, and utterly alone.

He decided the only thing to do was to walk out into the ocean and sink. He struggled to his feet, metal joints creaking, and waded deeper. He tried to cry, to scream, but no noise came out. His anguish remained bottled inside, like an unscratchable itch, fueling his hate.

The thought of taking one last look at the world did not appeal to him. He wanted to shut his eyes and sink beneath the waves. But he had no eyelids. He could not blink. So he stared across the water.

Floating on the surface, a few feet in front of him, was a soggy piece of paper.

With a sharp, robotic motion, Benjamin snatched the paper out of the water and held it up to his optical sensors.

"By every island and isthmus, by every archipelago, whosoever holds this document shall possess full ownership of THE 8TH CONTINENT."

Benjamin tightened his grip on the Ultimate Continent Ownership Form. Yes, of course. There was more to do. Much more. He could not sink to his eternal rest just yet. The Lanes had taken Benjamin's humanity away from him. He would have to return the favor.

First he would steal their continent.

Next he would destroy their family.

And then he would end their lives.

MATT LONDON (themattlondon.com) is a writer, video game designer, and avid recycler who has published short fiction and articles about movies, TV, video games, and other nerdy stuff. Matt is a graduate of the Clarion Writers' Workshop, and studied computers, cameras, rockets, and robots at New York University. When not investigating lost civilizations, Matt explores the mysterious island where he lives—Manhattan.

Find out more at
8THCONTINENTBOOKS.COM